# Willow Manor (Paranormal)

## Beau Bell

# Contents

# Chapter One

Katie had been the last person on the bus. She hadn't expected that. She knew Willow Grove was a small town—she had looked it up even before coming here. She'd even been here once. But she had been a small child then, excited and scared that she and her mom were picking up Grandma to come and live with them after Daddy was gone. She hadn't paid much attention to the town.

Even so, Katie had thought more people would be coming and going from the place. She didn't expect to spend the last thirty minutes of the trip with only the bus driver for company. And he wasn't much company, at that. When she'd told him she was going to Willow Manor for work, he'd shook his head and laughed humorlessly. "Good luck."

Any other efforts at conversation were wasted on his grunts and sighs. When the bus pulled into the small, dark terminal in the downtown area he turned to her before opening the door. "You sure you want to do this?"

"What do you mean?" Katie stood on the top step, clutching her purse to her side. "What's wrong with Willow Manor?"

"Nothing." He opened the door. "If you can sleep with your eyes open."

Katie frowned and stepped down from the bus to the sidewalk. She turned as the bus driver followed. "What's that supposed to mean?"

"Nothing." He grunted and walked down the side of the bus to the luggage compartment. "Don't mean nothing."

"It means something, or you wouldn't have said it." She followed him. "Is there something I should know about?"

"Just rumors." He pulled her two suitcases from the bus and shut the door. "I hear things, driving in and out of this place."

"What kind of rumors?" She followed him back to the front of the bus. "You can't ignore me the whole trip and then, when I'm finally at my destination, tell me something vague and ominous like 'good luck' and 'sleep with your eyes open'. What do you mean?"

"Look," He stopped and turned on the bottom step of the bus. He looked around, as if he expected someone to be listening. "Mr. Barrington employs a lot of people around here. And it's probably just a lot of coincidence. But there are a bunch of rumors. Just watch out."

"Rumors about what?" She frowned. Sexual harassment? Unfair labor practices? Unsafe working conditions? What was he talking about? "My grandmother lived most of her life in this town. I've never heard of anything bad going on here."

"Is that so?" The bus driver climbed up the steps and into the driver's seat. It was hard to hear over the motor, but as he shut the door, Katie thought he might have said, "Try not to die."

As the taillights of the bus disappeared into the night, the dark wrapped around Katie like a cold blanket. She shivered and went to rescue her bags from the shadows, bringing them into the light of the bus shelter. She looked around.

For all its quaint charm—the manicured tree lawn, the vintage black streetlamps, and just the general cleanliness of the downtown—Willow Grove was definitely the kind of place that rolled up its sidewalks at eight pm. The restaurant across the street, the clothing shops, the jewelry storeall dark, all closed. She checked her phone for the time.

Just after midnight. Well, of course everything would be closed. The bus trip took a lot longer than she had expected. Her itinerary said ten p.m. arrival. She looked around. Someone was supposed to meet her here. Mrs. Barrington had said someone would be here to pick her up. But there was no one.

"Oh, Katie." She pulled her bags closer to her under the bus shelter. "What have you gotten yourself into this time? Stuck out here in the dark, in a strange town, in the middle of the night, with no one here to pick you up."

She listened to the silence of the street. No cars on the road in a town like this. Everyone safe at home, probably long in bed. It was kind of peaceful, though. Not like where she lived, where there was always something going on somewheretraffic, music, conversationsno matter what time of the day or night.

"All alone." She said brightly, just to fill the void with sound. She glanced around for any sort of indication of which way she should start walking. Nothing. She frowned. "Talking to yourself."

She pulled out her phone and Googled 'Willow Grove taxi'. Nothing. 'Willow Grove Uber.' Nothing. It was like the town was straight out of the '50's. She tried 'Willow Grove Lyft.' Still nothing. "What the heck?"

Katie frowned. She searched the recent calls screen on her phone, looking for Mrs. Barrington's number. She hated to call so late, but she was expected. The bus had gotten in so late, maybe her employer assumed she had missed a connection. She would just have to let Mrs. Barrington know that she was here and

In the distance, a man's drunken singing echoed down the street. Katie looked around carefully. Her hand moved into her purse, closed around the can of pepper spray. Living in Baltimore these last four years had taught her to be careful.

The singing grew louder. Now she could hear footsteps. Pepper spray in her right hand and phone in the left, she hovered her thumb over the emergency call button. Then an older man came into sight.

Katie relaxed. He could barely walk and was singing some old song from the eighties about getting into the groove. There was no danger here, except to her eardrums, maybe. He stopped when he was almost upon her, as if he had suddenly noticed her.

"What?" He looked around fearfully. "What are you doing out here alone, miss? Don't you know it's not safe?"

"I'm fine." She assured him. "I just need to call my employer. Someone was supposed to meet me here."

"Oh, that sucks." He frowned. "They shouldn't do you like that."

"I'm sure it was just an oversight." She held her phone up. "I'm calling them now."

"I'll stay with you." The man wavered. He put out a hand to steady himself against the bus shelter. "So you won't be scared."

"I'm not scared. I'm fine." She smiled as she found Mrs. Barrington's number and hit redial. "It's ringing."

"You should be scared." The man's face grew serious, almost frightened, himself. "Scary things in the night."

Katie took a step away from him, instinctively. The phone continued to ring.

"Not me." He looked offended. "But, you know..."

"Yes, I know." She frowned. The phone went to voice mail. She kept her eyes on the drunk as she left a message. "Hello, Mrs. Barrington? It's Katie Gallagher. My bus was late, so I am at the bus stop here in town. I can't seem to find a taxi or Uber at this time of night. If you could please call me back and let me know that someone is on the way or if there is a hotel I should stay at tonight, I would much appreciate it. You have my number. Thank you so much."

The man had watched her intently as she left her message, looking alternately confused and elated. He barely waited until she hung up before he blurted out, "You're going to Willow Manor?"

"As soon as my ride arrives." She nodded. "I think there must have been some confusion on my arrival time."

"Very confusing." He said and took a step toward her. Katie backed up to keep him out of arm's reach and he fell, face first, onto the sidewalk.

"Oh, I'm sorry." She put a hand out for him. It had been a force of habit to protect her personal space. She hadn't meant for him to lose his balance. "Maybe you should sit down for a bit?"

"I gotta get home." He tried to climb to his feet. "My car is right over there."

"I don't think you should be driving." She frowned as he attempted to stand. "You're a little..."

"Drunk?" He laughed. "I'm a lot drunk, miss."

"Is there someone I can call for you?" She tried to encourage him to sit, but he kept trying to rise. "Someone to come pick you up?"

"He's not answerin' the phone." The man pointed at her phone. "I can drive it."

"That's not really safe." She argued. "Maybe you should"

"I can drive." He said and lurched to his feet. The momentum carried him a few steps before he stumbled and twisted around, searching. "My car is... somewhere."

Katie frowned. She moved to catch him before he fell again. He shrugged her off and pointed across the street to a newer luxury car. "There it is."

"That's your car?" She asked.

He nodded and fished an electronic key fob out of his front pocket. "Well, it's his car."

"Whose?" She took the key fob from him. The keychain was a leather tag with a gold metal B attached.

"Walter. My boss." He lunged toward the street and the car. "He gets mad if I don't bring the car back."

"I think he'd be angrier if you killed yourself in a car accident on the way." She frowned and followed him, just so he didn't fall again. "Why don't you take a nap in the car?"

The man laughed and opened the car door, crawled into the back seat. "You drive. I'm too drunk."

"I'm not driving you anywhere." She closed the door behind him. It was one thing to talk to a stranger at night, alone. It was a stupid thing, actually. But it was quite another to get into a car with one. "Good night."

"We're going t' the same place." He sat up in the back seat, looked confused about where he was. "Willow Manor. I work there. I live there."

"What?" She shook her head. He had heard her phone call. Was this some elaborate ruse to get her into the car?

"Walter Barrington." He said. Then, frustrated by her not understanding, he climbed over the back seat into the front and opened the glove box. He grabbed a paper and held it out to her, the car registration.

Katie opened the driver side door and took the registration from him. The car belonged to Walter Barrington. She glanced back at her bags, across the street in the dimly lit bus shelter. It was very late.

The man slumped against the passenger side door, the glove box still open. "Walter's my boss."

Katie sighed. This may be the dumbest thing she would ever do. "I need to get my bags."

"M'kay." He nodded. "I'll help."

"I've got them." She held a hand out to stop him. That was the last thing she needed to do, carry him back to the car again. "You sit."

In a moment she was putting the bags into the trunk of the car. She closed the lid and walked to the front. The man was still in the passenger seat.

"I'm Katie Gallagher." She said through the open window of the car. She held up her phone, where he could see. "I called my mom and left her a voice mail. She has a description of you and your license plate number, in case anything happens to me. Just so you know."

The man looked confused, then nodded. "That's smart. I'm Bill Allen. Nice to meet you Katie."

"I'll drive." She said as she got in and pressed the brake and ignition key. "You're a little"

"Drunk, yeah." He smiled and pointed down the road into a residential section. "That way."

"Am I headed the right way, Bill?" Katie said loudly. He had stopped humming some time ago and she was beginning to worry he had gone to sleep. They were well away from the downtown area, and fewer and fewer houses were out this way. "It seems like we're headed out of town."

"It's the right way." Bill stirred and sat up. Some of his drunk appeared to have worn off, although the smell of whiskey still filled up the car. Now that he was halfway sober, he was not as old as he appeared. He was maybe the same age as her fatheror as her father would be now. "You should be seeing it on the left any minute."

"So you work for the Barringtons?" She asked. "How long have you worked there?"

"Uh," Bill shifted in the seat, rubbed his face with his hand to clear his head. "I guess it's been about two years now."

"That's great." She nodded. "I'm going to be working for them, too. I'm the new nanny."

"I'm Mr. Barrington's handyman." He said.

"Oh, a handyman?" She looked at him, trying to sober up, straighten up. "Does the house need a lot of work, then?"

"Well, it's an old house. And there's a lot of property to take care of." Bill shrugged. "I drive for Walter sometimes, too."

"I can't wait to see it." Katie gazed out the window at the emptiness beyond. "It sounds amazing."

"Yeah." Bill laughed, but it was not a good laugh.

"It's pretty far out." She tried not to appear too worried, but wasn't this what crazy murderers did? Take you out into nowhere in the dark so no one can hear you scream? "Are you sure this is the right way?"

Bill chuckled and pointed out the window, over her shoulder. "That's all Barrington land there. Used to be farmland, back in the 1800's. Now, just waiting for the price to go up so it can be sold off to developers, I guess."

"Hm." Katie said. It was dark and she didn't really see any of that.

"It will be good for the kids to have a new nanny." Bill said. "It's been a while since the last one and they really don't like the public school."

"Oh? Why did the last nanny leave?" She glanced at him in the darkened car. "I wasn't told."

Bill didn't immediately answer. He seemed very concerned with his appearance all of a sudden, smoothing back his grey hair with his hand, tugging the wrinkles out of his shirt. He breathed into his palm, sniffed. Katie pretended not to notice all of that.

"And there's the woods." He broke the silence finally. "Goes from the road to the lake. The house is beyond the lake. The road wraps around."

Katie nodded. He seemed to know the area pretty well, at least. Maybe he killed all his victims out here? She laughed nervously. "That's a lot of property."

"Walter's rich." Bill shrugged. Then he sat up quickly and pointed to two stone pillars on the left. A metal gate hung open between them. "Turn here!"

Katie slowed the car and turned into the gated drive. The wrought iron arch above did, indeed, say Willow Manor. But the gate seemed to have been in mild disrepair for some time. Katie thought to herself that it was definitely something a good handyman should have taken care of by now.

"Walter is gone a lot for business." Bill said as they drove up the paved driveway. "It will be good for the kids to have stability."

"Oh?" Katie glanced around at the trees lining the road, creating a deeper dark around the car than just the night. "What does he do?"

"He owns a lot of hotels all over this part of the country." Bill pointed at the road ahead, indicating she should keep driving. "The Barrington Inns? I can't believe you haven't heard of them."

"Well, of course I've heard of that chain." She smiled, slightly relieved. The Barrington Inns were famous affordable luxury hotels. If she was being hired by the Barringtons, of course everything would be on the up and up. "I just didn't make the connection that it was this Barrington!"

"Yep." Bill sighed as the house came into view. Lights from the downstairs reflected off the lake. "Looks like Walter's still up."

"It's huge." She drove around the lake. The house was literally a mansion. She couldn't see the whole thing in the dark, but its outline was unmistakably large.

"Been in the Barrington family for over 200 years." Bill glanced up at the façade as Katie parked the car in front.

"Wow." She opened the door and got out. All fear had evaporated, leaving only excitement and curiosity. "So Mr. Barrington grew up here, too?"

"Yep." Bill pulled himself out of the car. "And his father. And grandfather. And great"

Katie laughed in surprise and awe.

He shrugged, held his hand out for the key fob. "Well, you get the idea. They're old school rich."

They walked up the elaborate brick sidewalk to the double-doored entry. At the top of three half-moon steps, the doors seemed even more elegant and impressive. They were solid, dark wood, ornately and tastefully carved with blooming roses and vines.

Katie touched the smooth wood gently. It felt strong, old, and filled with hundreds of stories about the residents it protected. Everything about it spoke of luxury and class and, she smiled wryly, money. This one door likely cost more than she made all last year.

"I'll let Walter know you're here." Bill said as he turned the key in the front door. "Then I'll come back and get your bags out of the car."

"Don't bother." Katie nodded as he held the door open for her and indicated the foyer with his hand. "I can get them, Bill."

"Bill!" A man's voice bellowed out of the room off to the side of the entry. "Where the hell have you been? I've been looking all over for you!"

"Sorry, Mr. Barrington." Bill stepped into the double doorway of that room. The light from that room cast a long shadow into the entry behind him. "You said I had the evening off, so I"

"Yes, well. Be that as it may," The man, Walter Barrington, was obviously annoyed. "I was looking for you and you weren't here."

"Sorry." Bill said softly. He glanced back at Katie, in the entry, as if he were going to introduce her. "I"

"There's been another... incident." Walter was gruff, upset. "Marcus Jones was here again."

"Again?" Bill forgot all about Katie. "Why?"

"Why do you think?" Walter snapped. Then he seemed to gain control of his emotions. "It's very difficult for me when you're not here to back me up. And I just can't afford to have to deal with that. Not when there's a reviewer coming in a few weeks. And when so many people have just left the company."

"Not because of..." Bill glanced back at Katie. She took a step forward, but he shook his head at her very slightly.

"Of course, because of that!" Walter growled. He mumbled a few things Katie was unable to hear. Then he sighed loudly. "And to top it off, they're all getting hired away by RPR."

"But..." Bill turned his attention back to Mr. Barrington again. "I thought Roger P. Reynolds died?"

"Yes, but apparently his widow is charge now. I've never met her, but it seems like she's after me personally." Walter grumbled. "She's been outbidding me on convention contracts, purchasing prime real estate in my markets, and negotiating exclusivity contracts with large corporations with whom I've dealt for years. She's hiring even my long-term hotel managers right out from under me."

"Wow." Bill shook his head, looked down at the floor. "She's more aggressive than Roger ever was."

"She's ruthless! And she's out for blood." Walter shouted. Then he seemed to calm himself a little. "And all of this... you know... other... is making me lose sleep."

"I'm sorry, Mr. Barrington." Bill said, with sincere sympathy. "It won't happen again."

"Yes," Walter growled, but he seemed to have lost his fury. "Well, see that it doesn't."

In the awkward silence, Katie gestured to Bill to introduce her. Bill lowered his eyebrows and shook his head minutely. Katie nodded and pointed to the room. Bill frowned and shook his head again.

"Good God, Bill! What is wrong with you? Why do you keep wobbling your head like that?" Walter bellowed. "Have you been drinking again? So help me..."

Katie took the opportunity to slip into the room, in front of Bill. She smiled her best. "Excuse me, Mr. Barrington, my name is"

"And what have I told you about bringing your drunken waitresses home?" He interrupted. He seemed shocked and offended by her very presence. "There are children in this house."

"Whom you will awaken, if you continue to shout." Katie said calmly.

Mr. Barrington ignored her, turned his fury to Bill. "Do you think there's another employer in this town who will put up with this kind of behavior? It's as if you want me to fire you!"

"Mr. Barrington, I" Bill fumbled.

"Now wait a minute, Mr. Barrington." Katie raised her voice slightly. "You can't talk to people like that. Bill has been nothing but kind and I"

"I'll talk however I wish in my own home." Walter snapped. "But I will not be lectured by a barmaid barely out of her teens."

"I'm twenty-six y" Katie stopped, gained control of her emotions. That was the key to dealing with children, or adults, for that matter. Control your own self first. She took a deep breath and began again with a softer, more congenial tone. "Look, I was hired by Mrs. Barrington to be a nanny for"

Both men startled. Bill looked miserable, but Walter became angry once again.

"Mrs. Barrington?" He was a dangerously quiet kind of angry. "There is no Mrs. Barrington."

"What do you mean?" Katie frowned. "I spoke to her on the phone three days ago, when we made the final preparations."

"Impossible." Walter waved her off.

"I'll show you." Katie pulled her phone out of her purse, found the recent calls screen and hit redial. A soft buzzing sound emanated from Walter's suit pocket.

He retrieved his phone, looked at it incredulously. "What? How did you get this number? Was that you who drunk dialed me this evening?"

"I didn't drunk dial you." She insisted. "I hit redial from Mrs. Barrington's number from when she called me on Monday. Like I did just now."

"Impossible." He looked sick. "You're a liar."

"I don't lie." Katie was insulted. "Maybe your wife just didn't tell you?"

Bill spoke softly. "Katie, maybe you should"

"Bill, are you listening to this?" Walter was both angry and upset. "What were you thinking, bringing her here like this?"

"I couldn't leave her there on the street, Mr. Barrington. Not wh en..." Bill insisted. "It's not safe. What was I supposed to do?"

"Look." Katie showed him her recent calls page. The number showed up four times over the last three weeks. "I spoke with Mrs. Barrington several times."

"What nerve you have, Miss Gallagher." Mr. Barrington's anger was fading, becoming something else. "My wife has been dead for over two years."

"Mr. Barrington, I" Katie was too shocked to respond further. What did he mean Mrs. Barrington was dead? That couldn't be right.

Bill stepped up, put his hand out. He stopped short of touching Katie's arm. "Look, it's late and everyone is tired. Can't we sort this out in the morning?"

"Yes." Mr. Barrington seemed distracted, distraught. "Drive Miss Gallagher back to town please, Bill. Put her up in the Inn."

Bill frowned slightly. He glanced at Katie, then back to Walter. "I don't think that's a very good idea, Mr. Barrington. It's late and... you know..."

"Fine." Walter seemed almost defeated. "I suppose you'd like to stay here tonight, Miss Gallagher?"

She hesitated. There was something very odd going on heresomething that set off a whole lot of alarm bells in her headbut, she really did need a place to stay. And she really did need this job. She smiled, hoping that the expression would sooth all of them. "Yes. I would appreciate that very much."

Mr. Barrington nodded. "Bill, see that Miss Gallagher gets settled into one of the guest rooms."

"Yes, sir." Bill smiled now, too, an expression of nervousness.

"We'll sort this out in the morning." Walter repeated. Then he turned and exited the room. "Good night, Miss Gallagher."

"Wow. He was really rude." Katie shook her head once Walter was gone. "Is he always like that?"

"Yeah." Bill shrugged. He seemed to have calmed down quickly. "That's what comes from having more money than anyone else your whole life."

"I know it's not my place to ask, but what's going on around here?" Katie hesitated awkwardly. She was prying, she knew, and she hated to pry. But there was definitely something unusual here. "Who is Marcus Jones and why would you have to 'back Mr. Barrington up'?"

Bill sighed and looked away, as if he were formulating a neutral answer. "People like Walter just aren't used to not being in control of their world. I'm sure he's just overreacting."

"He seemed pretty agitated." Katie insisted. "What kind of incident was he talking about?"

Bill shrugged, but the casualness of the gesture didn't reach his eyes. "I don't know. He's just stressing out. That's just how these rich folks are. It's nothing."

"It didn't seem like nothing. He seemed very upset." Katie could not leave it alone. She pressed. "And who was it who hired me, if Mrs. Barrington is gone?"

"Maybe it was Miss Bonham before she left." Bill shrugged again. "Come on. I'll show you to the guest room and then I'll go get your bags from the car."

The guest room was larger than any room she'd ever had, including her room at her last employer, the Culvers. It might have even been larger than the Culvers' living room. It was tastefully decorated with a contemporary teal color palette that worked surprisingly well with the antique woodwork of the room. A beautiful pale brick fireplace filled one wall, its walnut mantle covered in a light sheen of dust, and its mouth filled with a huge dried flower arrangement.

A queen sized four poster bed rested between two large windows, covered with rich, satiny curtains. On the opposite wall, an enormous empty wardrobe awaited her few meager belongings. Katie touched the bed, tested it with her hand. The mattress was firm, but soft. The comforter was thick and billowy.

Bill entered, dropped her bags by the door. "Here you are, Miss. You'll be safe here."

Katie turned at the odd phrase. "What do you mean, I'll be safe?"

"What? Oh." Bill chuckled self-consciously. "I meant, you know, sleep safe and sound."

"What?" She startled. "You said it again!"

"It's just an expression. I'm sure you've heard it." He was embarrassed. "Sorry. I'm not college educated like you or anything."

"No, I'm sorry, Bill." She forced a smile. There was no reason to take it out on Bill, who had only been kind to her. "I'm just a little on edge tonight. A mystery phone call. Hired by someone who apparently doesn't exist. It's all very weird, don't you think?"

Bill smiled, turned toward the door. "It's okay, Miss. You're safe here."

She frowned. There it was again that word, safe. What was going on here?

"Well, good night then, Miss Gallagher." Bill shut the door behind him.

"Good night, Bill." She said to the door. The room felt suddenly emptier.

# Chapter Two

At first, Katie wasn't sure what had woken her. She rolled over and picked up her phone from the bedside table, checked the time. Three in the morning. She had been asleep less than two hours. Then she heard it againa voice, soft and low, and very close. Her heart beat a little faster, a little harder. She had the distinct feeling that something was not right, that she was not alone.

Katie held her breath and leaned forward to listen. It sounded as if it were coming from inside her room. It was definitely a woman's voice, but if there was no Mrs. Barrington and no Miss Bonham, who was it? It sounded too adult to be one of the children. Stranger still, even though the voice was faint, she could swear it was saying her name.

"Katie." It was little more than a whisper, but not quite a moan. "Katie..."

Katie flipped on the lamp next to the bed and scanned the room for the source, but there was no one there. Still the voice continued to vocalize, albeit softly, and with difficulty. She listened more carefully, trying to determine its owner. Her initial fear began to give way to curiosity. "Hello?"

"Katie..." The woman said so softly, Katie nearly had to strain to hear her. Then, it seemed to gather both strength and volume. "Save them!"

This directive was so forceful that Katie jumped out of the bed, half from shock and half from concern. If she had any doubt the voice was real, it would have evaporated with that last statement. That was very definitely a demand and it was very definitely meant for her.

"Where are you?" Katie walked to the door. She listened. Nothing. She opened the door a crack. Light from her room cut a swath across the hardwood floor of the hall. There was no one there. "Hello?"

The house was completely quiet. The voice had been loud enough to wake Katie, so why was no one else in the hall? Surely that last statement—Save them—was sharp enough to make someone take notice, sleeping or not. Katie took a step out into the hall. The oak planks felt cool against her bare feet. She stood listening, waiting.

There was no sound at all. Not even a whisper of air from the air conditioner or the sound of crickets from the outdoors. The house was certainly well-built and well-insulated. She took a step or two down the hall. No light shone from under the other doors, no sounds from within.

And no ghostly voice, either. Katie sighed. She knew she hadn't imagined it. "Hello?"

Suddenly, the door to her left opened, and Walter Barrington stepped into the hallway in front of her. He seemed startled by her presence and closed his robe reflexively. "Miss Gallagher, what are you doing outside my bedroom?"

Katie blushed involuntarily. She had not thought to wear her own bathrobe, so she crossed her arms over her chest for propriety's sake. "Mr. Barrington, I—did you hear that?"

"Hear what?" He narrowed his eyes suspiciously.

"I don't know. I was sleeping and something woke me up." She cast her eyes around at the shadows in the hall, not quite dispersed by the glow of the lamp from inside her room or the small guide lights set into the baseboard of the hallway. "I came out here to see what it was."

"You heard something in the hall?" Walter stiffened. He seemed unsurprised, but also somewhat bothered. "I supposed you've heard all the stories about this place. I'm well aware of what people say. Well, then"

"Yes. No." She frowned and collected herself. "I mean, that's not what's happening here. I heard an actual voice. I thought it was in my room, but there was no one there. So I thought I must have misheard. I came out into the hall to look for the source."

"A voice." He was not convinced. He raised his eyebrows, as if daring her to insult him with some wild rumor. Katie wondered if this obvious pride in the face of what he must think was criticism was behind the bus driver's warnings. "Well, who was it?"

"I don't know." She met his gaze. "It was a woman, I think."

"Hmph." Walter's face set. He looked over his shoulder and down the hall at the closed doors. "Someone was talking out here? A teenaged girl, maybe?"

"No." She shook her head. "This was definitely a woman."

"A woman." He frowned. "What woman? Who was she talking to?"

"I don't know." Katie really did not. "To me, I think."

"To you?" He was curious now. "You're a stranger here. What did she say?"

Katie frowned. If she told him, he wouldn't believe her. "I think she said save them."

"I see." Walter relaxed. He nodded his head as if he had her all figured out. "You've heard all the stories about the haunted Barrington house and the crazy Barringtons. All that worked on your subconscious and you had a dream."

She shook her head. He might have had a point, if she weren't so absolutely sure she had been awake to hear at least some of the voice's communication. "I don't think so."

"Then one of the children. Clarissa has been staying up all night and sleeping all day." He shrugged. "Typical teenager."

Sure. Maybe it could have been a teenager, Katie thought. But something in her gut told her it wasn't. And why would Walter's teenage daughter stand outside her room at night and say Save them? It didn't make sense.

There was only one explanation that made sense, but Katie discarded that one as soon as it crossed her mind. Years of her mother's derision regarding her "overactive imagination" had made its mark on her. So, while she might think she was seeing or hearing something that only a child would believe, she was a logical, rational adult and was able to quickly banish such nonsense.

Still, she knew she had heard a voice. She just had to determine a logical, rational explanation for it. "It seemed like an adult."

Walter seemed intent on dissuading her. "Perhaps it came from Bill's room, then? Maybe he's brought some woman home from the bar."

"I'm pretty sure he was too drunk to go back out. He's probably sleeping it off." She frowned, remembering Walter's comment about drunken waitresses. "Does he bring overnight guests often?"

"No. No." Walter said. "Never. Bill is devoted to this family and wouldn't think of disgracing it."

"Well then." Katie shrugged. "Whose voice could it be?"

"A dream." Walter seemed to satisfy himself with that answer. "Brought on by the strangeness of tonight's eventsthe phone call, the late arrival in town, Bill..."

"She woke me up." Katie said. Then the look on his face told her he thought she was being foolish. It was the same look Mom gave her every time she mentioned... She checked herself. "I suppose I was dreaming."

"Most likely." He nodded, satisfied in his own mind. "Get some sleep, Miss Gallagher. It's been an interesting evening, to say the least."

Just then, the door at the end of the hall opened. A young, dark haired girl exited with more stealth than Katie would have thought possible. The girl carefully closed the door and turned around, not to the right, where Katie and Walter were standing, but to the left, where there was only a darkened window. She started to move toward the window.

"Clarissa!" Walter's voice was sharp. "What are you doing up?"

Clarissa started, whipped around to face them. Her face was pale and slack, as if she didn't fully comprehend the environment. Then her demeanor changed suddenly, as if she were waking from some sort of trance. She looked around and the fear was evident in her expression. She had not known where she was or what she was doing before that very moment.

The girl's disorientation and confusion were evident in the tears that formed in her eyes. She blinked them back and affected an angry aloofness that Katie guessed was more of an act than actual attitude.

"Nothing." Clarissa said quickly. Then she took a more critical look at Katie and Walter, both in their pajamas in the hall. Her lips twisted in disgust. "Who the hell are you?"

"Go back to bed, Clarissa." Walter said sternly. He pointed at the door.

"Yes, sir." Clarissa tossed an exaggerated salute, then reluctantly turned and went back to her room.

Katie stood awkwardly, as Walter ensured his daughter did as she was told. Then he turned to her and sighed as if that were an explanation. "My oldest."

Katie nodded. "She's about fourteen or fifteen?"

"Fifteen." Walter frowned. "Worse than the terrible twos."

Katie was concerned about the way Clarissa looked. Her skin was very grainy and pale, with dark circles under her eyes. She didn't look at all well. "Has she been ill?"

He frowned even deeper. "She doesn't sleep much these days, I'm afraid."

"I can tell." Katie nodded. "I think it's affecting her health."

Katie walked a few steps down the hall to the window. She looked out over the back garden. The moonlight illuminated the patio area, cast deep shadows into the landscaping beyond. Katie stared into those shadows. Was that a person? Or just a weird shape created by the trees and plants? She shivered involuntarily.

Walter came up behind her, looked over her shoulder. "What is it?"

"Nothing, I supposed." Katie turned away from the window. "I thought I saw something. A person."

Walter stared out the window for a few seconds, giving Katie the chance to observe him. He was trying to project an air of casual non-belief, but she could tell by the way his eyes scanned the yard that he was deeply worried. She wondered what had happened to make him feel so guarded. He turned back to her abruptly and his expression registered some slight surprise to find her observing him.

"Seeing things? Hearing things?" Walter smiled wryly. "Careful. This is beginning to be like Miss Bonham part two."

"Nothing like that." Katie smiled uneasily. "Just tired, I guess."

Walter seemed to think about something for a moment. Then he asked, "Did you bring your credentials, Miss Gallagher?"

"Yes, of course." She was momentarily caught off guard. "I can get them right now."

"No, no." Walter shook his head with a smile. "Tomorrow morning will be fine. For now, get some sleep. Delia, at least, will be up early."

"Thank you, Mr. Barrington." Katie smiled. "I will."

"We'll talk about your future here, tomorrow after breakfast." He turned and opened the door to his own room. "Good night."

"Oh, thank you! Good night!" She smiled broadly. Then she returned to her own room, happy and excited. Never mind that she still didn't know who had hired her. Or what was happening here. Or who had been calling her name at three am.

Inside the room, she glanced around uneasily. She tried to be logical, rational. But she knew what she had heard. She addressed the unseen voice. "Hello? Are you still here?"

No answer.

"Good work, Katie." She whispered to herself. "Half a night in a new place and you've lost it already.

# Chapter Three

The rest of the night passed without incident and Katie woke and dressed by 7:30. She came downstairs and realized she had no clue where she should be. No one was around, so she followed the hall beyond the sitting room, past the dining room, to the kitchen.

The room was enormous, and fancier than any home kitchen Katie had ever seen. Beautiful wood cabinetry lined the walls, with built in fixtures. One wall boasted a wide paned window. Katie was struck by the sheer elegance of the room. She ran her hand over the granite counter on the island in the center of the room and gazed up at the copper-bottomed cookware hanging above it.

"Hello?" A man's voice startled her from behind. "Can I help you?"

He was standing in the doorway of a pantry, with a jar of honey in one hand and a box of tea in the other. He was dressed in a white button-down shirt, jeans, and a bibbed apron. He was positively ancient.

"You startled me." Katie smiled and offered her hand. "I'm Katie Gallagher. I'm the new nanny."

The old man looked at her hand, then gestured with his own two full hands. He looked at her suspiciously. "Nobody said nothing about a new nanny."

"I know. There was some confusion." She said. "I arrived last night."

"Last night?" He seemed to try and ascertain her sincerity just by staring at her. Then, he either decided she was telling the truth or he decided it didn't matter. He shrugged. "Well, fine. You don't have any food allergies, do you?"

She was surprised at the quick change of subject. "Uh, no."

"Not some kind of vegetarian?" He narrowed his eyes. Katie shook her head. "Gluten free? Lactose intolerant?"

"No." She said. "Nothing like that."

"Alright then." The man crossed to her, put the tea and honey down on the island and offered his own hand. "My name is Archie Morris. I'm the head cook here."

"Pleased to meet you, Mr. Morris." She shook his hand, surprisingly firm and warm despite the man's frail appearance, and gave the large room another admiring look. "How many cooks does Mr. Barrington employ?"

"It's just Archie, Miss." He winked and grabbed the kettle off the cook island and took it to the sink. "And there's just me. But I like to say head cook. Makes me feel important."

Katie laughed. "Of course. Then I am the head governess. And it's Katie."

"Don't go getting airs, Katie. You have to put in some time here before you become head of anything." Archie put the full kettle on the burner and turned it on. "You can't just come in last night and start out at the top this morning."

"I apologize." Katie stepped back out of the way while Archie moved to the oven and removed two tins of muffins. She could smell the warm cinnamon and apple from her place at the island. "Those smell delicious."

"They are delicious." He stripped off the oven mitts and dropped them onto the counter. "I've made these at least twice a week since Walter was a boy. They're his favorite."

She watched him move around the kitchen with a smooth grace that came from years of familiarity. "So you've been here a long time, then?"

"Oh yes." He opened a cabinet and pulled a large bowl out. Then he went to the refrigerator. "I worked for Mr. Brandon Barrington since I was a young man. Now, I work for Mr. Walter Barrington."

"That's awesome." She smiled. The old man was not just loyal to his employer. He had a real affection for Walter Barrington. "You're just like one of the family."

"I am one of the family, Katie. I'm not just like one." He moved to the counter with the bowl, a carton of eggs, milk, green and red peppers, and plate of ham. "Walter may pay me to cook here, but that's got nothing to do with how he feels about me or how I feel about him."

She felt her cheeks color. She had insulted him. "No, of course not. I didn't mean to imply..."

"Let me tell you something about Mr. Walter Barrington, Katie." Archie cracked the eggs into the bowl with a quick, purposeful motion. "My wife, Masie, used to do the housework around here... make the beds, clean the floors, that kind of thing."

"I see." Katie listened. His words were soft and unhurried, but she could feel their importance, nonetheless.

"Then she got sick. Cancer." Archie whipped the eggs with a fork. "That's an expensive disease. We didn't have that kind of money."

"I'm sorry." She said softly.

"But Walter... He says, 'Don't worry about money. Just worry about getting better, Masie.'" Archie choked on the words. He pulled a pan down from a rack as he collected himself. "Walter paid for everything. I never saw a single bill."

Katie swallowed the growing lump in her throat. "That's very generous."

"It's not generosity, Katie." He chopped at the peppers. "That's just how he is. He would do anything for his family."

"Thank you for telling me that, Archie." She could not help but be impressed with the affection and respect that underscored his words. "That makes me feel very good to work here."

"You should feel good, Katie. You should be happy." Archie paused and looked down at the knife, his mind far away from green peppers. "Let me tell you something else, Walter and Charles Barrington and my son Elvin all grew up together, in this house. Close as brothers. Then Elvin, he got killed in Iraq two months before Alicia was due."

Katie opened her mouth to say she was sorry for his loss, but he waved her off.

"When my grandson, Elvin Jr., was born, Walter set up a college fund for him, investments and stuff. By the time Elvin graduated high school, he had enough money to go to school wherever he wanted." The old man looked up from his work, his expression serious. "Walter said he didn't want Elvin to ever feel prohibited by money. He said there were so many other things for a young man to worry about, money was the easiest thing for him to fix. Now Walter was a young man himself, just out of college. Just after his own dad passed on. And he's thinking of others like that? That's rare. Let me tell you."

"I'm glad to hear this, Archie." Katie took a step closer. Whatever the circumstances of how she came to be here, she was beginning to feel like she belonged hereor at least, she wanted to belong here.

"That's why it makes me so mad when people talk about Walter like they do. Walter's a good man. He doesn't deserve what they say about him and he doesn't deserve that bully Marcus Jones coming out to harass him all the time." Archie chopped the pepper with a ferocity now that made her step back again. "Don't nobody better say anything bad about Walter around me, that's all I got to say."

Katie was encouraged by his fierce loyalty.

"Do you... ah... do you know what happened to the last nanny?" Katie tried. Archie turned from his work and raised one eyebrow disapprovingly and she immediately felt censured. "I'm not gossiping, I'm just trying to determine the best way to approach my lesson plan. If I knew what was going on with the children..."

"The children need someone. That's for sure. With their mama gone and all." He said slowly, deliberately. Then he seemed to decide what he wanted to say. "Miss Bonham was a nice lady. Very sweet-tempered and kind. Like you. But I don't think Miss Bonham was able to handle a house with a history like this one."

"What do you mean?" Katie watched him fold the peppers into the eggs. Rather, she watched him watch her as he made the eggs. He seemed to be waiting for some reaction.

"This place has been around for over 200 years." Archie poured the eggs into the pan. He glanced at her out of the corner of his eye as he worked. "It's got stories. It's got spirits."

She couldn't decide what reaction he was waiting for. Was he trying to frighten her? What was the point in that? "You mean ghosts?"

"Oh yes, ma'am. Ghosts. And plenty of them." He laughed. "When you have a 200-year-old house, you've got spirits for sure."

She watched him cook while she tried to figure him out. Why would he be so adamant about the kindness of the Barrington family, so defensive about the wrongs they suffered from misinformation and uninformed opinion, and then tell her the house was haunted?

"Miss Bonham saw them, I think. She wasn't emotionally equipped, as they say, to handle it." He didn't turn to look at her this time. "I can tell you've seen them, too. The question is, are you emotionally equipped to handle it?"

Katie started. The mysterious voice of last night was still working on her subconscious. She had not wanted to acknowledge its origin, even to herself. But she had known, from the first time she heard it, that's what it was. She had just trained herself not to name the sensation for what it wasghost. What would Mom say if she knew Katie was hearing things again? Or that she was casually tossing around the G word with a complete stranger? "I"

"Who the heck are you?" A boy of about twelve demanded.

Katie turned, disoriented by and grateful for the interruption. "Hello. I'm Miss Gallagher. I'm--"

"Why are you here?" The boy frowned deeply. "Did my father invite you here?"

She bent slightly, to bring her face to his level. "I'm your new"

"Mom?" His face darkened with pain and anger. "No way. I don't need a new mom, so you can"

"Blake!" Archie turned and gave him a stern look. Blake stopped talking abruptly.

"I'm your new nanny." Katie explained.

"So I don't have to go to school in town anymore? Awesome." Blake's face calmed instantly. "And we don't have to deal with Miss Bonham anymore? Bonus!"

"That's a little rude to talk about Miss Bonham like that." Katie admonished. "What do you mean by that, Blake?"

"Miss Bonham... Coo-coo. Coo-coo." He rolled his eyes. Then, seeing she was not amused, he shrugged. "It was funny at first, but then it just got scary."

"That's..." Katie frowned. She studied the boy's face. His face held emotion, but his eyes didn't. He seemed almost lifeless without the anger.

He looked at Archie. "Can we have waffles?"

"Ham and eggs, muffins, and strawberries." Archie said firmly. "On the table in a couple of minutes. Go sit down."

"Fine." Blake nodded to Katie. "I'll save you a seat next to me."

"No, sit next to me, Miss." A little girl strolled into the kitchen. "Arabella says you're a nice one."

"Well, hello there." Katie said. "I'm"

"Katherine Elizabeth Gallagher." The little girl put out a hand to shake, a strangely adult gesture. "You're the new nanny, if Daddy lets you stay."

Katie smiled, curious. "How did you"

"Arabella says you and her will be friends." The little girl's attention drifted to the counter, where a bowl of strawberries sat, unattended by Archie. "Not like Miss Bonham."

"It's nice to" Katie started, but the girl cut her off.

"Arabella says you know a lot of games and you're more open minded than Miss Bonham." The little girl inched toward the counter with the strawberries.

"Well, I hope" Katie was cut off again.

The little girl snaked a hand up to the counter and into the bowl. "Arabella says I should give you a chance."

Katie smiled. "Is Arabella a friend that lives nearby?"

Archie turned and gave the girl a stern look. She pulled her hand back and laughed.

"Pretty sure Arabella wants you to go get ready for breakfast, Delia." Archie handed the girl a strawberry. "You'll have plenty of time to talk to Miss Gallagher about Arabella later."

"Okay." Delia stuck the strawberry in her mouth and left.

Katie turned back to Archie. "Who is Arabella?"

Archie frowned. "She's been talking to Arabella since her mama, Diedre, passed on."

"I see." Katie nodded. She looked up as Clarissa entered the room and stopped at the sight of Katie.

"Good morning, Clarissa. It's nice to see you up so early." Archie said as Clarissa regained her composure and strode purposefully to the refrigerator. "Breakfast in two minutes. Please take a seat in the sunroom."

"Whatever." Clarissa said under her breath. She gave Katie a dark look. "You're still here?"

"Hello, Clarissa." Katie put out her hand. "I'm Miss Gallagher."

"Don't care." Clarissa looked at Katie's offered hand disdainfully. "You're too young for him, though."

"I'm sorry, what?" Katie was taken aback.

Clarissa frowned and spoke slower, as if to a child. "You're too young to be dating my dad."

"I'm not..." Katie laughed awkwardly. "I just met your father last night."

"Gross." Clarissa made a disgusted face. "That makes it worse."

Katie shook her head, confused. "Clarissa, I'm not sure where you got the idea"

"Oh, I'm sorry. Did I not see the two of you in your pajamas in the hall together last night?" Clarissa crossed her arms over her chest as if she were daring Katie to dispute it.

Archie raised one eyebrow at that.

"We were in the hall because we each heard a noise that awakened us." Katie tried not to be offended. "Turns out, that noise was you trying to sneak out of the house."

Clarissa harrumphed.

"I'm not here for your father, Clarissa." Katie said. She kept her voice even and reassuring. "I'm the new nanny."

"What? Another one? Are you going to flip out too?" Clarissa shook her head. "This is so stupid. Why do we even need a nanny? Walter!"

She stormed out of the room.

Archie looked at Katie pointedly. "You and Walter?"

"No. Not at all." She shook her head vehemently. "I don't know why he was up, but I heard..."

"You heard what?" Archie seemed curious, not suspicious.

Katie lowered her voice automatically. "A woman's voice."

Archie considered that for a moment. "In the hall?"

"Yes." She nodded. "Or in my room. I don't know."

Archie turned back to the eggs and began scraping them into a serving bowl. "What did this woman want?"

"I don't know." After all his talk of ghosts, Katie was sure Archie would believe her, but she still felt uneasy about saying anything. "Mr. Barrington thinks I was dreaming."

"Hmph." Archie said. He loaded a cart with breakfast and began pushing it to a small room off the kitchen.

"What, hmph?" She followed him. "What do you mean?"

Archie shrugged, as if the answer were obvious. "You're hearing the ghosts of this place."

"No, I don't..." Katie stopped as they entered the sunroom. Warm autumn light shone through the windows, which made up most of three walls. She could see a thick woods to one side and what looked to be a small cemetery on the other. Blake and Delia sat quietly at the table, while Bill read a magazine. Walter entered from the hallway, followed by Clarissa.

"That's enough. I didn't ask for your opinion on the matter. Just sit down." Walter said to Clarissa. Then he saw Katie. "Good morning Miss Gallagher, Archie, Bill, children. Let's enjoy breakfast, shall we?"

Breakfast was awkward. Katie listened as Delia talked to no one about her dream about catching fireflies by the pond. Blake and Clarissa stared at their plates. Walter texted most of the time. Only Bill seemed to notice Katie was there, asking her a few questions about places she had previously lived and worked.

After the children were excused, Walter put his phone down next to his coffee cup and gave her a long look. His aloof expression didn't change at all, except in his eyes. They progressed through several minute alterations as he thought. Then he abruptly picked up the phone and left the room, saying "Bring your credentials to my study, Miss Gallagher. We'll talk."

"Of course. I'll get them." She glanced at Bill, who looked equal parts nervous and happy. Then she excused herself to retrieve her papers.

Walter was waiting for her in his study. He shut his laptop when she entered and stood. "Ah, Miss Gallagher."

She smiled warmly, Archie's declarations of loyalty and affection still fresh in her mind. It was important to her, in a way that she hardly understood, that this man liked her. "Please, call me Katie."

"Katie, fine." He gestured to a chair in front of the desk. "Please sit."

"Thank you." She sat demurely. She handed him a folder. "Here are the references and qualifications you asked for."

He barely flipped through them before handing them back to her. He didn't seem interested enough to even read them. "Fine. Well that all appears to be in order."

"But you hardly looked at them." She tried to hand them back. Her credentials were impeccable. She had been extremely well liked at her last position and they had written a very favorable recommendation. She was a little disappointed that he was not more impressed.

"I've seen enough." He sat back down. He kept his eyes on her, but his expression remained guarded. His voice softened. "The main thing is, you're correct. My children do need...supervision. My business is very demanding. I have to travel often. I'm not always able to be a hands-on parent."

Walter's gaze dropped to his desk and he took a moment to collect himself. When he spoke again, she could hear the pain in his voice, the grief and self-recrimination still fresh enough to give him pause. "My wife, Diedre, was always the one who managed their day-to-day activities. I'm a poor substitute, I'm afraid."

Katie could see now that his grief was vast and lonely, that his cold, angry manner was an affectation. It was merely a mechanism, meant to protect his injured heart. "Mr. Barrington, I"

"No, it's true. I've had to juggle work and home for these last two years. I've had to rely on nannies and drivers and maids to watch my children while I work." Walter drew a deep breath and, with it, drew strength enough to reequip his emotional armor. He spoke directly, watching her face for reaction. "It's a difficult thing to entrust their welfare to others. Especially when the person entrusted with such a sacred duty... turns out to be undeserving of that trust, like Miss Bonham. Do you understand what I'm saying, Katie?"

She did. He could not bear another betrayal. "Of course, you need to know you can trust me."

"Exactly. Because, while my business is very demanding, there is nothing more important to me than my children." Walter paused for emphasis. "Nothing."

Katie did not look away from his stare. Though he tried to hide it with his abrupt manner, she felt his true meaning. His family was everything. That sentiment struck such a nerve with her that she nearly choked up before answering, "I can assure you, Mr. Barrington, that your trust in me is"

"Yes. I know it's well-placed. I get a good feeling about you, Katie." Walter turned and looked out the window. "I know you won't let me down."

Katie nearly stood. "Oh, Mr. Barrington, I"

"Yes, I know. Before you get too eager..." He turned back to her. His face softened again. "There are... things you should know about my children."

"What kind of things?" Katie asked carefully.

"As I mentioned, my wife is gone. We haven't had a nanny for a while, since... Miss Bonham left. And there were a few others." Walter sighed deeply. "Let's just say it's been a rough two years for this family."

"I'm so sorry for your loss." Katie said softly. "May I ask, how did your wife die?"

It was the wrong thing to ask. Walter's face changed abruptly. His eyes grew hard and his mouth turned down in a twisted grimace of pain and anger.

"That's a private family matter!" He said harshly. "None of your business!"

"I'm sorry." Katie felt her cheeks redden. "I didn't mean to pry."

Walter seemed to take a moment, during which he wrestled his own emotions. Then he spoke again, softer.

"I apologize for snapping at you. It's just..." He tried to formulate the best way to say something. "My concern now is for the children. Delia was so young she doesn't even remember her mother. But Blake is depressed and angry."

Katie nodded. She had witnessed that upon first meeting Blake. "I'm sure that's very natural in this situation. Maybe I can get him to open up to me?"

Walter nodded. Then he frowned even deeper. "Blake is not the problem."

"Oh?" Katie raised both eyebrows. "But I thought you said"

"It's Clarissa." He said quickly. "My oldest."

"Yes." Katie was sure Clarissa had gone straight to Walter after their meeting this morning and complained about Katie's presence. "We officially met this morning."

"It was nice to see her before lunch." He said, with some relief. "She's been staying up all night and sleeping later and later. It's beginning to affect her health. You mentioned yourself how pale she was when you saw her last night."

"Has she seen a doctor?" Katie offered. "She does look a bit anemic."

"Yes." Walter frowned. "That's what the doctor said, as well. He seems to think this is something teenage girls doskip meals and stay up late."

Katie frowned. From what she had noticed this morning, Clarissa didn't have any issue with eating. "Have you talked to her about it?"

"Yes, of course I talked to her." Walter was indignant. "I told her she can't act this way. It's childish and reckless."

"That's not what I meant." Katie said. "Have you talked to her about why she's acting out this way? Children usually have a reason for what they do."

"She has a reason." Walter huffed. "She's a spoiled 15-year-old. Everything is so dramatic. Every interaction is an affront to her personal autonomy."

Katie frowned. "Fifteen is a difficult time for a girl, Mr. Barrington. Especially without a mother to"

"Yes. She reminds me continually that her mother is gone. As if I'm somehow at fault." He glanced out the window again. These words were obviously difficult for him to face. "As if she believes all the..."

Walter's voice trailed off. He continued to look out the window. If an artist were to ever paint a portrait of a hopeless and despondent father, this would be the inspiration.

"Maybe she just needs someone to talk to?" Katie said softly. "The death of a parent is a very difficult thing. Have you considered a grief counselor?"

"Absolutely not!" Walter's gaze snapped back to her. "I won't have the whole town talking about 'that crazy Barrington family'!"

Katie frowned. "I'm sure no one would say that."

"They say it now." He shrugged desperately. "Miss Gallagher, you have no idea how people in this town like to gossip."

"Maybe it would help if I talked to her?" Katie offered.

Walter shrugged and turned back toward the window. He seemed lost in thought until Katie spoke again.

"Do you have any of the previous nanny's progress reports I could review?" She asked. "It would help me establish where I need to start with lessons."

"No." He sighed. "Unfortunately, Miss Bonham left quite suddenly."

"I see." Katie nodded. "Do you mind if I ask why she left?"

"Yes. As a matter of fact, I do mind." Walter turned toward her again. He looked tired. "But since you will most likely hear from Clarissa anyway... I'm certain she was on drugs."

"Oh no!" Katie was shocked. "While she was responsible for the children?"

"Yes." Walter shrugged. Then he waved a hand, as if the details were unimportant. "Well, it was drugs or alcohol or some sort of mental illness."

Katie shook her head. "I don't understand."

"She was prone to...shall we say, hallucinations." Walter put his hands up dramatically, as if he feared the very air. "Something dark and evil was stalking this family. She was told by the spirit world she had to save us all. Powerful forces were at work."

He frowned. "It became so disruptive to daily life that the children dreaded their lessons. Poor little Delia became convinced Miss Bonham wanted to steal her away."

"Oh my!" Katie frowned. No wonder the children were so distrustful of her. They'd had such a traumatic experience with their last nanny. And no wonder her nightmare last night upset Mr. Barrington so much. She must have reminded him of his terrible experience with Miss Bonham. So, regardless of what she thought she heard last night, she resolved to keep it to herself. She forced a smile. "I will get started with lessons right away."

"Good. Thank you, Katie." Walter breathed a sigh of relief. "I'll have Bill send the children to the library for you."

"Thank you, sir." Katie almost gasped out loud at the thought of a private library and how casually Walter mentioned it. That was certainly a characteristic reserved for the rich. She smiled as warmly as she knew how. "I want you to know you can count on me. I will care for your children like my own life depends on it."

"Of course." Walter nodded. Then, he looked around the room, a little lost, and began packing up his laptop in its bag. "God, I'm late. Excuse me. I have to get to the office now. Please tell Bill to pull the car around."

Just then, the doorbell rang.

"Who the devil is that?" Walter frowned. "Excuse me, Katie."

"I'll get it." She offered. "You're busy."

"I am. Thank you." He agreed. He went back to zipping his case. "I'm sure it's nothing good, the way things have been going lately."

Katie walked down the hall to the front door. Poor Walter, she thought. Hopefully I can help this family feel better again.

She opened the door to a thirtyish blonde man in a well-tailored suit. His blue eyes met hers immediately, and the smell of his cologne was intoxicating. She felt drunk, just standing near him. He was, by far, the most handsome man she had ever seen in her life and it took her a second to realize she was staring. He seemed as surprised to see her as she was to see him.

"Hello?" Katie collected herself quickly. She couldn't help the blush that burned her face and neck. "Can I help you?"

"I hope so." A broad smile stretched his face. "I'm Adrian Chesterfield. And you are... a relative of the Barringtons, perhaps?"

"No." She laughed. Why was she blushing, anyway? Could she be more awkward? "I'm"

"Not Walter's girlfriend? Or... oh no. Not Bill's?" He made an exaggerated pained expression. "Please say no?"

"Adrian." Walter appeared in the hall behind her. His chastisement was fake, and covered a slight smile, belying the friendship between the two men. "Miss Gallagher is the new governess."

"Oh?" Adrian raised his eyebrows and smiled broadly. "Miss Gallagher, is it?

"Watch out for this one, Katie. I believe all the women in the office are in love with him." Walter closed the distance between them. "What's up, Adrian?"

"I needed to let you know about something before you get to work."
The younger man glanced at Katie, then raised his eyebrows at Walter.
"Something to do with... current events."

Walter frowned and nodded. He gestured toward the study. "Come
in, Adrian."

When she located Bill, he was on his way out the back door.

"Bill, guess what?" She called. "I'm staying!"

"Good." Bill nodded, but he didn't look as happy about it as she'd
thought he'd be.

Katie was confused. Bill seemed to be her only ally in the house so
far. Why did he look so disappointed? "What's wrong?"

"Nothing, Katie. It's just..." He looked around, then lowered his
voice. "Are you sure that's what you want to do?"

"What do you mean?" She laughed nervously. Why was he sending
her such mixed signals? "Of course it is."

"Yeah, I know." Bill shrugged. He seemed like he was holding back.
"It's just... "

"Say what you mean, Bill." She crossed her arms. "Why wouldn't I
want to be here?"

"You seem like a nice lady, is all." He said. He started to move around
her toward the door. "And this place isn't always what it seems."

She blocked his way. Why did everyone in this place insist on creating such mystery? Why couldn't they just come right out and say
whatever it is they didn't want to say, but really did? "What's that
supposed to mean?"

Bill seemed to take a moment to collect his thoughts. "Look, Walter's not a bad guy. He's a little snobby, is all."

Katie shrugged. She had already figured Walter out. "I'm not bothered by"

"But people around town don't like him, Katie." Bill said bluntly. "That tends to rub off on people who associate with him. I just wouldn't want you to be, you know, lumped in with the rest of us."

"What do you mean? I thought you said the Barringtons had lived here more than 200 years?" Katie shook her head.

"Yeah." Bill said. "For 200 years, they've been the rich folk in the mansion."

Katie frowned. "I see how that could"

"But DiedreMrs. Barringtonwas one of us. She grew up in town. Went to public school." Bill smiled a little, thinking of Mrs. Barrington. Then the smile melted into a sad expression. "In fact, I think the first time she ever left this town was when she went to college."

"I see." Katie said, but she didn't. How would that make people hate Walter?

Bill continued. "She got her accounting degree, came home, and immediately started working for Walter."

"And that's how they met?" Katie smiled. It was the meet-cute trope of half the romance novels she'd ever readsmall town girl captures the heart of the billionaire next door.

"Yes. He had just inherited the family business a few years before and she was fresh out of college. They started dating." Bill smiled wistfully. "They did make a good-looking couple. If Walter had kept any of her pictures up, you would see."

Katie looked around. In fact, she hadn't seen any photos of Mrs. Barrington in the house. "Why aren't there pictures up?"

Bill didn't answer. He frowned, as if he were remembering distasteful things. "Deirdre's parents were livid when she started dating Walter."

"They didn't like him? Why not?" Katie's attention was drawn back to Bill and his story.

"The rich are very different from the rest of us, Katie." Bill said.

She frowned. "I don't believe that."

"It's true." He nodded. "They have different priorities. They look at things differently. They don't worry about the same things we do."

"They just have more money." She shook her head at his classism. "They're not alien creatures, Bill."

"All I know is, she'd never been anywhere before and then, all of a sudden, he was taking her to Paris, to The Bahamas, and to New York." He shrugged. "People thought he wore her like a beautiful jewel on his arm."

"That sounds lovely." She countered. "It sounds to me like they had a lot of fun together."

"Those of us who know him, know he loved her." Bill said bluntly. "But other people... let's say people thought he was only using her."

"Using her?" She scoffed. "He married her!"

"Yes. He did." Bill seemed almost vindicated. "And her parents and everyone else had to admit they were wrong about Walter."

"Good!" Katie exclaimed.

Bill sighed. "And then she was killed."

"Killed?" That information was a little shocking. "I assumed she was ill."

Bill shook his head. "No. It was... very tragic."

"A car accident?" She felt even more sorry for Walter. To lose the love of your life so suddenly...

"No." Bill looked down at the ground. His expression was absolutely miserable. "She was murdered."

Katie gasped. "Oh my God! That's terrible! But why would that make people hate Walter?"

"Because..." Bill lowered his voice. "They all think he did it."

"Oh, poor Walter." Katie felt her own heart break now. "Is that why he's so...?"

"Yeah, wouldn't you be?" Bill shrugged. "Wife dead, kids acting out, nanny freaking out..."

She shook her head. "Poor Walter."

Bill frowned. "And then to be treated like a criminal on top of all that..."

"But that's just all gossip, right?" Katie didn't understand. "If the police really suspected him, they would arrest him, right?"

"It's complicated." Bill took the car keys off the wall next to her. His sigh was deep and filled with complex emotions. "Just... don't believe what they say about Walter. I know he's innocent."

"Wait..." Katie reached out as he brushed past her to the door.

"I know he's innocent." Bill nodded. Then he went out the back. "I gotta bring the car up.

# Chapter Four

Katie looked around the large room, filled with shelves of books. Several expensive-looking paintings hung on the walls. The furniture was elegant, old world plush. In the center of the room, Blake and Delia sat at a large oak table, playing games on their iPads.

"Wow." She turned in place, taking it all in. She felt like Belle at the castle of the Beast. "This is an impressive room."

Blake mumbled, "It's boring."

"Boring?" She laughed. "It's wonderful! So many books!"

"That's what makes it so boring." He didn't even look up from his game.

"I love it." She challenged him. "I would spend my whole day here."

Blake laughed wryly. "That's what makes you so boring."

Delia closed the cover on her tablet. She was more willing to engage with Katie than her brother. "Most of these books are very old. Arabella says some of them came from Europe with the first Barringtons. She says I'm lucky that I can read. Back in her day, girls were supposed to just sew and cook. Arabella says she didn't even go to school. She says her father wouldn't allow it."

"You mentioned her before." Katie stepped close to the little girl and smiled. "Is Arabella one of your friends from town?"

Delia laughed, genuinely amused. "No, Miss Gallagher. Arabella lives here."

The sound of a video character crashing made Blake close the cover on his iPad, too. "Arabella is Dumb Delia's imaginary friend."

Delia stood and stomped her foot on the plush carpeting. "I'm not dumb! And Arabella is real!"

"Blake, that is not a nice way to talk about someone." Katie intervened. "How do you think that makes your sister feel?"

He shrugged. "Bad, I guess."

"And sad." Delia sat down, dejected.

"How would you feel if someone else said that about your little sister?" Katie said.

Blake's face reddened with anger and he pounded the table with a fist. "I would punch him in the face!"

"Well, maybe not that." Katie used her tone to calm Blake. "But don't you think you should tell Delia something?"

He looked at his sister and his expression softened. "I'm sorry, Delia."

"It's okay, Blake." Delia forgave him instantly. She looked up at Katie. "But Arabella is real, Miss Gallagher. She's the one who told me you were coming."

"And how did she know that?" Katie laughed. "Apparently no one else did."

Delia shrugged. "I don't know. Arabella just knows things. She says you're good and that you will help us all be happy together. Not like Miss Bonham. Arabella didn't like her at all. She said Miss Bonham wanted to steal us and never come back."

Katie frowned, remembered what Walter had said about the governess wanting to take the children away.

Blake laughed. "Miss Bonham. Coo-coo! Coo-coo!"

"Not nice, Blake." Katie warned. "We've discussed that."

Blake laughed. "I know. Sorry."

"Well, let's get started on lessons, shall we?" Katie looked around the room. "Where is Clarissa?"

Blake opened up his tablet and loaded the game again. "She's probably sleeping."

Delia nodded somberly. "She sleeps a lot."

"Hm. Well we saw her this morning at breakfast. She couldn't have gone to sleep so quickly." Katie said. "Why don't we get started here and I'll see if I can find her after that?"

Blake shook his head but didn't look up from the game. "No way. I'm not doing school stuff if Clarissa doesn't have to."

Katie sighed. "Don't worry, Blake. No one's getting out of schoolwork."

Katie knocked firmly on Clarissa's door. She could hear music playing from the room beyond. But no one answered. She knocked again.

Clarissa's voice was the tone of a bored, annoyed teenager. "Go away. Nobody's home."

Katie frowned and opened the door. Clarissa was on the floor, leaning back against the bed, watching a video on her phone.

"Clarissa," She said firmly, "I need you downstairs in the library for lessons."

"Yeah." Clarissa didn't look up. "I'm not going."

Katie stood for a moment, waiting. When Clarissa didn't move, she sighed. "Clarissa, it's time for schoolwork. Your father has hired me to teach and care for you and your brother and sister. And that's what I'm trying to do. The lessons are part of it."

"I don't believe Walter hired you." She gave Katie a withering gaze. "Walter doesn't care whether we go to school or not. When we went to school in town, I skipped every day. Every. Single. Day. He didn't even notice until he got a call from the principal. I don't know why you're here, but I know it's not because of Walter's fatherly love."

"Of course your father loves you." Katie was a little surprised at what Clarissa had said. Could that be true? Walter didn't notice? "I'm sure he's just really"

"Busy. Yeah. That's what he says." Clarissa finished. The anger in her voice did nothing to cover the hurt, though. "Too busy to notice when his daughter skips school 10 days in a month? Too busy to notice his son is on the edge of a nervous breakdown? Too busy to notice his youngest child talks to ghosts more than her own family? And don't get me started on you governesses. Miss Bonham and her crazy ghost séances or whatever... That just made things worse. It's no wonder mom left us. I'd run away from here, too."

Run away? Katie was confused by that phrase. Why would Clarissa say run away?

She said gently, "Clarissa, I"

"Save it." She waved a dismissive hand at Katie. "You don't care either."

"Of course I do! I care about all of you!" Katie knelt next to Clarissa on the floor. "I know you don't know me yet, but I'm a good person. I really am. And I really want to take care of you and Blake and Delia. I want you to know how special you are and I'm going to make sure you don't ever feel neglected again."

"Oh, please. You don't care." Clarissa looked away from her, but Katie could hear the sadness catch in her throat. "It's just your job. You get paid to act like you care."

"You're wrong, Clarissa. I just need to find a way to prove it to you. I hope you'll start to think of me as one of the family and not just an employee." Katie stood and held out her hand to Clarissa. "You know what? I suspect you haven't enjoyed school up until now because you haven't been intellectually stimulated. But we'll fix that. Now let's go down to the library and see if we can find something you like."

Clarissa grudgingly got to her feet, but she ignored Katie's offered hand as she stood. "Whatever."

Downstairs, Bill was just about to head up the staircase.

"There you are, Clarissa. You're supposed to be in the library." He said. "I've been looking all over for you."

Clarissa crossed her arms. "Did you look in the bottom of a whiskey bottle, Bill?"

"Clarissa!" Katie was shocked by her rudeness. "That's no way to talk to anyone. Please apologize to Mr. Allen."

"Sure." She shrugged. "If he apologizes for being drunk all the time. And trying to sneak back into the house in nothing but his underwear."

"Clarissa." Katie warned.

"Well, he didn't look very hard." Clarissa frowned. "I was in my room."

"You little…" Bill shook his head. "That was the first place I checked. You weren't there."

Clarissa laughed. "Imagine that. Maybe I went for a walk?"

Bill crossed his arms, too, now. "Maybe you were out in the gardens, smoking again?"

"Maybe." She shrugged. "What are you going to do? Tell Walter on me again? You know he doesn't care."

"Maybe." Bill countered. "I could tell him you're giving Miss Gallagher trouble about going to school."

"Fine." Clarissa countered. "And I'll just tell him about your little extracurricular activities."

"You don't scare me." Bill said, although it seemed like he was a little nervous about what she might say.

Katie intervened. "Clarissa, that's not what I asked you to do."

"Fine. I apologize." She said with an exaggerated sigh.

"Thank you." Katie said. "And thank you Bill for your help."

Bill looked very upset. "No problem, Miss Gallagher."

Katie mentally shook her head. There were so many things going on in this household. It was going to be a monumental task just to wrap her head around it. First things first, though. She looked at the girl sternly. "Now Clarissa, we'd better get to the library and get started."

"Hold up a sec, would you, Katie?" Bill seemed a little uneasy.

"Sure." She motioned to Clarissa toward the library. "Go on ahead, please. I'll be right there."

Clarissa looked at Katie, then Bill. The she rolled her eyes as she walked away. "Whatever."

Katie turned to Bill. "What is it? I thought you were driving Mr. Barrington this morning?"

"He rode with Adrian." Bill shook his head. Then he looked down at the floor. "Listen, about all that stuff... You should watch her pretty carefully. There's something off about her."

Katie laughed knowingly. "Well, she's 15, so she's got a lot of emotions right now. Anger tends to be one of the most dominant feelings in teens, unfortunately."

"Yeah." Bill frowned. He shuffled his feet a little. "It's not just that."

Katie nodded. "And she is still dealing with the loss of her mother."

"Look, Katie, she's not wrong. Last week she caught me trying to sneak back into the house." Bill looked up at her. He looked miserable at his admission. "I... had been out drinking all night."

Katie sighed sadly. "Oh Bill."

"And I was in my underwear." He said, ashamed. Then he looked up, quickly. "But she only knows this because she was trying to sneak back into the house, too."

Katie was a little shocked. "Didn't you tell Mr. Barrington?"

"No. Again, she's not wrong." He frowned. "I've told Walter about some of the stuff she tries to pull off. Like the time he was out of town and she took his Porsche for a joyride. Or the times I caught her smoking in the family cemetery."

"Hm." Acting out was usually a cry for attention. Coupled with Clarissa's assertations, it was clear there was a disconnect between Walter and his children. "What does he do about it?"

"Poor Walter. He gets so much hate from the townies... and the police..." Bill shrugged. "I think he just wants to avoid the drama at home."

She frowned, a little disappointed. "So he does nothing?"

Bill nodded and shrugged. "Basically."

"Well, that's going to stop." Katie said firmly. "Children need boundaries. That's how we, as adults, provide them with a safe environment to learn."

"I'm glad to hear you say that, Katie." Bill seemed to struggle with finding the words for what he had to say next. "There's something else... Have you noticed the marks on her neck?"

"What?" She hadn't. "What marks?"

"I saw them last week when she was sneaking into the house." He indicated his neck with two fingers. "On the side of her neck, red and bruised."

"Hickies?" Katie shook her head. Clarissa was only 15. "Do you think she's meeting a boy when she sneaks out?"

Bill shrugged uncomfortably. "If they're hickies, they're like none I've ever seen. They were bleeding."

She frowned. "Then what?"

Bill's silence was awkward.

"You can say it." She assured him. It as obvious there was an adversarial relationship between Bill and Clarissa. "I won't let anyone know it came from you."

"Do you believe there are supernatural things in the world?" He blurted.

"What? Like ghosts and goblins?" Katie frowned. She wanted to hear more. She wanted to tell Bill about the voice at night. But she didn't want to become a Miss Bonham. She heard her mother's words come out of her mouth. "No, of course not. I'm not a child Bill."

"Look, if you stay around here, you're gonna hear stories." He said, as if he were giving her valuable information. "You're gonna see stuff that will make you believe the stories."

She narrowed her eyes. She'd already heard enough innuendo and half-stories to get her interest up. "What kind of stories?"

"Stories." Bill nodded knowingly. "Like, about how this house is haunted."

Katie held her tongue. Did Bill know? Had he heard the woman's voice? She said softly, "Those are just stories, right? It's like you said, people gossip. They make things up."

"Well, there have been stories about this place as long as it's been here." Bill agreed. "I remember my Grandpa Bob telling me about one of the old-time Barringtons. Went crazy and tried to drown her kids."

"That's awful!" Katie said. Then she smiled knowingly. "But you know he probably told you that so you didn't play near the pond."

"Maybe. There seems to be an accident every generation." Bill shrugged. "Walter's little sister drowned in that same pond."

Katie was uncomfortable thinking that the voice she heard at night in her room could be that of a child killer. "You really think this house is haunted by a murderous ghost?"

Bill looked like he was going to say something else. Then he just shrugged. "Listen, Katie. I've seen so much around here. I really wouldn't doubt any of it."

She shook her head. So, was Bill saying there was a ghost? Or that there wasn't? "What do you mean?"

Bill shook his head and started down the hall toward the door. "Nothing. You'd better get to your lessons before those kids wreck the place."

"Bill wait!" She said, but he didn't turn.

What could he have meant by that.

# Chapter Five

"Katie, finally!" Mom's voice was calm, her words precise almost to the point of sounding mechanical. Katie looked at the time. It was only 4:30 pm, yet Marietta Gallagher was already drunk enough to be extremely careful with her words. That was the thing about high-functioning alcoholics. They knew how to be careful, seem normal. They knew how to make it seem like everyone else was overreacting to their drinking, if you called them out on it. "You didn't call me when you arrived, dear. I was worried about you. Especially after that crazy voicemail you left me."

"I'm sorry." Katie said. She did feel guilty about not calling right away, especially after leaving a message that she was driving a stranger's car to a strange house in a strange town with a strange man. She had pretty much forgotten about that. "It was very late when I got here. After midnight."

"Hm. That was over sixteen hours ago." Mom said. Katie could hear ice clinking in a glass near the phone. "So I suppose you didn't have access to your phone until now?"

"Well, I am working." Katie frowned. She wanted to say, why didn't you call me, if you were really worried? But she didn't. That would only start a fight, and she knew she could never win a fight with Mom. "I'm sorry. This is the first chance I've had to call you."

"At least you're alright." Mom said after several seconds of silence. Then, when that didn't get a reaction, "I was worried."

"Sorry to worry you." Katie said again. She thought about this morning's conversation with Walter Barrington. He'd told her his children were of the utmost importance to him, that he would do anything to protect them. By contrast, Katie had called after midnight to tell her mom she was getting into a car with a drunk stranger, and her mother had not bothered to call to check on her. The difference would have hurt if she weren't so used to it.

"How do you like it there?" Mom asked, but Katie doubted she wanted to hear a detailed answer. There was another clink of ice.

"It's nice." Katie laughed a little self-consciously, trying to lighten her own mood. "Hey, you know what? I didn't realize it, but these are the Barringtons from Barrington Inns."

"Really?" Mom seemed impressed, finally. "Well, that's something. Is it all champagne and caviar then?"

"Hardly." Katie laughed a little. "My job is to take care of the children here, remember."

"Oh well." Mom paused to take a sip. "I'm sure they entertain some important people. They probably have senators and movies stars over for dinner regularly. Maybe you'll meet a rich husband."

"Mom." Katie frowned into the phone. "I'm not"

"I know. I know." Mom tried to minimize the offense by changing the subject. It was that famous Marietta Gallagher verbal aikido that made people feel like they were being too sensitive, if they objected to her emotional attacks. "Have you had a chance to meet any of your Grandmother's relatives yet? They're supposed to be some kind of muckety-mucks in that area."

"No." Katie mumbled. The phrase itself was not necessarily offensive, but she could hear the contempt for her father's side of the family in her mother's voice and it bothered her. "Like I said, I've only just gotten here."

"Yes, I know. And you're taking care of the children." Mom sighed. This was all just so much tiresome detail, so ordinary. "So besides all that, how is it going?"

"It's going pretty well, all in all." Katie said. "But..."

"But what?" She could almost imagine Mom leaning forward in her chair now, keen to hear something juicy.

"It's just," Katie sighed. She had no idea why she wanted to tell her mother. She knew it would not be taken well. Still, she couldn't help it. She had no one else to talk to. "There are all these stories about this house being haunted and"

"Katie." Mom snorted, her tone dripping with derision. "You don't still believe in all that mystical crap, do you?"

"No, of course not." Katie said quickly. But she did. She had never stopped believing. She'd just learned not to talk about it, since Mom found it so ridiculous. And why did she still crave her mother's approval, anyway? She was a grown woman. Still, she continued. "But, I did hear something weird..."

"Like a rumor?" Mom was paying attention once again. "Interesting. What was it? Was it juicy?"

"No, like..." Katie hesitated. She knew what Mom's reaction would be, but she couldn't stop herself. "Last night, when I was asleep, I heard a woman's voice calling my name."

Mom seemed disappointed. "A dream?"

"No." Katie chewed her lower lip. She should stop right now, before the inevitable fight. She was only fueling her mother's disapproval.

"It was a dream." Mom was bored with the conversation now. "You said yourself you were asleep."

"No, I mean, I was asleep, but then the voice woke me up." Katie was beginning to regret bringing it up.

"Someone in the house? Mrs. Barrington? The upstairs maid?" Mom laughed wickedly, her attention renewed. "The downstairs maid? A mistress?"

"No. It was weird." Katie had to explain now. She couldn't bear the thought of her mother thinking ill of Walter. "As if she were right there in the room. But no one was there."

"Sounds like you dreamed it." Mom was disappointed once again. "You shouldn't tell people your dreams, Katie. Dull people and weirdoes do that."

"I'm not a" She stopped, checked her temper. She was not a weirdo. She knew that. And she knew that, if she called her on it, Mom would act as though she were being attacked. She would claim she never called Katie a weirdo, she merely said that she was acting like one. Her mother would treat the whole conversation as if she were the injured party, being unjustly accused of name calling and there would be a long, painful fight until Katie ultimately apologized. She sighed and spoke calmly. "I'm not the only one who's heard it. The previous nanny had heard the voice too."

Mom was quiet for a moment. Then, she yawned audibly and there was a clink of ice again. "Well, I give up then. You heard a voice. What is the big deal?"

Katie blurted it out, even knowing what her mother's reaction would be. "Mom, I think it was a ghost."

"Oh, that again." Mom said flatly.

"No, not like before." Katie protested. Her cheeks burned at the memory of the last time she told her mother she'd seen a ghost. Her mother had made her watch horror movies every night before bed, just so she would understand the difference between fantasy and reality-Mom's homemade version of immersion therapy. "This was real."

"Katie, look. You've got a good job. This is a rare opportunity to get in with someone who has some real influence and money." Mom's tone was direct and almost caustic. "You don't want to lose this because of your imagination."

Katie protested weakly. "It's not my"

"Yes. Yes, it is. Just like before. You were dealing with your beloved grandmother's death, dealing with the stress of being the one to find her. And your mind played tricks on you." Mom said, in the condescending voice she mistakenly thought was a comforting tone. "This is the same thing. You've had some stress dreams, brought on by a new situation and new people. And, no doubt, fed by these ghost stories about their old mansions that I'll bet these rich folk get a kick out of telling people."

Katie sighed. "I don't think so."

Another clink of ice in the glass. "You know I'm right."

"It's just..." Katie gave up, fell silent.

"Well then just come home." Mom said, as if she were done with the whole conversation. "Tell Mrs. Barrington it's not a good job fit for you and just come home."

Katie frowned. Another one of her mother's famous overreactions. "No, I don't want to"

"Well make up your mind, sweetie." Mom said impatiently. "Stay or go."

"Of course I'm going to stay." She said, as firmly as she could, given the fragile state of her self-worth.

"Okay then." Mom said and suddenly she was happy again, as if their previous conversation hadn't even happened. "Call me tomorrow, okay?"

Katie spoke softly, defeated. "Okay."

"And get some sleep. You're more susceptible to stress when you're tired." Mom said. Then she took a serious, semi-motherly tone. "And Katie, you can't be talking about ghosts if you want to stay employed with influential people."

"Okay. Bye Mom." She rolled her eyes and sighed.

Mom hung up without saying goodbye.

Katie frowned at the screen. Why did she do this to herself? She knew Mom would be like this. She should have just texted her, short and sweet: Made it here. Everything is wonderful. Talk to you soon.

Honestly, that would have satisfied her mother's "worry" and it would have avoided all the stress she was feeling right now. Katie sighed, put the phone back in her pocket, and went downstairs to spend some time in the library before dinner.

Five-year-old Katie sat in the middle of the bed and stared at the toy rabbit. It wasn't a play-with bunny, it was a look-at bunny. Grandma had made it for her when she was a baby. It was a lifelike grey fur rabbit with a pink dress, a feathered hat, and rhinestone and pearl earrings, necklace, bracelet, and ring all glued on. Grandma had named the toy "Madame Fluffbottom Cottontail," because she'd said a fancy rabbit needed a fancy name. But Katie had started calling it Grandma Fluff as a toddler, and the name stuck with her.

So now she sat on the bed, picking at Grandma Fluff's glued on jewelry and missing Grandma. The adults were talking downstairs-sometimes sad, sometimes laughing at some happy memory. And meanwhile, Katie was left to deal with her loss alone.

And then, the most amazing thing happened. Grandma was standing at the foot of the bed. Katie was so happy, she bounced up onto her knees and held out her arms for a hug. But Grandma didn't lean in for a hug. Instead she just stood there and smiled down at Katie. She seemed both happy and sad at the same time. She was saying nothing, but Katie felt like she wanted to tell her something.

"Grandma! You're awake!" Katie was relieved and happy that her mother had been wrong. When Katie had found Grandma sleeping on the floor, she'd tried so hard to wake her up. Even after Mom had pulled her away and told her Grandma could not wake up, that she had died, Katie had screamed and cried for Grandma to get up. Mom had been adamant that Katie would never be able to talk to Grandma again and yet, here was Grandma. So someone was wrong about that.

"How did you get here?" Katie was confused. Grandma said nothing. "Mom said you were far away."

Grandma smiled and rolled her eyes. She reached out her hand toward Katie.

"Grandma?" Katie drew closer. Grandma opened her mouth to speak but no sound came out.

She stretched out her own hand, almost touching Grandma's fingers. "Grandma?"

Grandma seemed to be trying to talk, but there was no sound.

"Grandma?" Katie said, just as their fingers connected. A warm tingling wrapped around Katie's hand like a comforting touch.

And then, very softly, Grandma spoke. "Katie.

# Chapter Six

"Katie..." The woman's voice came from far away, and yet somehow it sounded as if it were in the room with her. Katie sat up in bed. She looked at the clock on her phone. Three am.

"Katie." There it was again, a little stronger. She concentrated on the voice as she lay quietly. She tried to determine exactly where it was coming from.

"Who's there?" Katie whispered into the dark. If she could just determine who the woman was—who the ghost was—or what she wanted, Katie could...

What? What could she do? She had never been able to do anything for Grandma. She'd never been able to find out what it was Grandma had wanted from her. What good was it to see ghosts and not be able to understand why they appeared to her?

"Katie." The voice seemed to try and gather strength. "Save..."

Katie switched on the lamp and glanced around the room. Everything was in place. She threw off the blanket and stood, looking around. "Hello? Arabella? Is that you?"

There was no answer, but the room grew suddenly colder. Katie walked to the door, opened it. Soft light from the hall night lights flooded in. Those lights were motion sensitive, so that meant someone had been in the hall. Were ghosts able to set off motion sensors? She stepped out onto the rug. "Hello?"

A sudden movement drew her eye to the end of the hall. As Katie walked that way, she began to make out Clarissa's form by the window. She was partially hidden behind the curtains and seemed to be just staring out the window.

"Clarissa, what are you doing up?" She said softly.

Clarissa came out from behind the curtain slowly. Strangely, she seemed a little confused, but she covered it by frowning. "None of your business."

"What are you doing?" Katie glanced over the girl's shoulder and out the window. The patio below was dark and the pale first quarter moonlight cast strange shadows from the ornamental shrubs and trees of the yard. She saw no one in the yard, but every instinct in her said that there was. "Who's out there?"

Clarissa rolled her eyes. Her face got paler, as if that were even possible. "I don't know what you're talking about."

Katie frowned. She put her hand on Clarissa's shoulder, led her away from the window. "What are you doing up? Are you sneaking out?"

"What do you care?" She shrugged Katie's hand off.

"I do care." Katie sighed. With just that brief contact with the girl's shoulder, she could feel Clarissa trembling slightly. Fear? Or just cold? "Where were you going at this time of night?"

"Ugh. Why are you even here?" Clarissa rolled her eyes again and tried to get by her.

Katie searched her face. Despite her tough, don't-care façade, Clarissa looked even more sickly than before. She was not sleeping because she was sneaking out. But why was she sneaking out? Who was she meeting? And how could Katie stop it? It was a dangerous activity, to be sure. Who was she meeting? Who knew what that person's motives were? Clarissa was only fifteen. She did not have the life experience to anticipate another's intentions.

Besides all that, the lack of sleep was clearly affecting Clarissa's health. Katie could tell just by looking at the girl's skin. But all of this—the surliness, the secretiveness, the anger—was most likely caused by the underlying depression she was suffering. If she could get Clarissa to open up to her, Katie was sure she could help. And she was sure that whatever was going on with Clarissa, the sneaking out at night would stop.

But now was not the time to have that conversation, in the hall at three a.m., in their pajamas. This was something Katie would have to do some reading on and prepare. It was something she would have to discuss with Walter.

Katie took Clarissa's arm gently. "Go back to bed before you wake your father."

Clarissa's jaded face belied the misery in her eyes. "Walter doesn't care about me."

"He most certainly does." Walter emerged from his own room, wrapping his robe tightly. "Now I suggest you do as Miss Gallagher says and get back to bed."

Clarissa seemed momentarily surprised. Then she scowled and stomped off. "Fine!"

Walter waited until Clarissa shut her bedroom door. Then he turned to Katie. "Thank you, Katie. I had suspected she was sneaking out. Now that we know she is, we need to put a stop to it."

"Agreed." Katie glanced out the window once more at the empty garden. There was no one there. She was sure of it. But she had an eerie feeling, almost subconsciously, that she was wrong. "I think she was meeting someone outside. She was looking out the window."

"Hm." Walter gazed out the window, searching the shrubbery with his eyes. "I'll have Bill go out and take a look around with me."

"I can go with you." Katie offered. "I'm already up."

"No, that won't do." Walter shook his head. "You need to get some sleep to care for Blake and Delia in the morning. I'll have Bill do it."

Katie grimaced, pained at the thought of being the cause of Bill having more to do. "That doesn't seem fair to Bill. Doesn't he also have work to do in the morning?"

"Nonsense. Bill will help me search." Walter started down the hall. "I'll go wake him and tell him now."

Katie sighed. Poor Bill. Walter really expected a lot from him. She was pretty sure most of what Bill did around here fell far outside of the handyman job description. Still, she told herself silently, Bill was a grown man and could make his own decisions. He didn't need Katie to butt into his business.

Katie stepped closer to the window and scanned the empty garden once again. There was no one there, but she couldn't shake the feeling that her eyes were deceiving her. Some unnamed sensation itched at her brain, twisted her stomach. She couldn't even describe the feeling to herself. It felt as if she, herself, were being watched, as if she had looked out the window a split second after that person had ducked behind a bush or a tree.

She shook her head to clear her thoughts, think more rationally. She turned and let her eyes drift down the hall toward Clarissa's room. There was no light under the door, no sound from within. She had gone back to sleep as if the encounter had never happened.

Clarissa's behavior was, perhaps, the most curious part of the incident. She was awake and about, but she seemed just as surprised by that as Katie was. And, though she tried to act defensive about it, when Katie asked her about who was in the garden, Clarissa had seemed startled, almost frightened. And, though she grumbled at being caught in the act, she certainly gave up and went to her room without much of a fight. Indeed, there was so little drama, she seemed almost relieved to be caught.

Katie frowned. Who was Clarissa meeting? Where was she going? Willow Manor was too far away from town for a person to be out walking. A person would have to have a car to get here. Was Clarissa planning to get into a car with someone?

She took another look out the window at the garden below, just in time to see someone looking up at the window. He was young, maybe just a little older than Clarissa. He saw Katie and smiled curiously before ducking back into the bushes. Katie gasped and ran toward the stairs. She had to tell Walter and Bill.

Bill and Walter beat back the bushes in the garden. They combed the lawn with their flashlights. They covered the area down to the pond and out to the road. They found no trace of the young man.

"I don't see anyone out there." Bill said as the three of them met back up on the patio. "Are you sure you saw someone?"

"Yes, positive." Katie insisted. She pointed at the ornamental box-wood spirals. "He was right there. Looking up at the window."

Bill cast his flashlight around once more. "We probably scared him off."

"If he comes around again, I'll do more than scare him off!" Walter fumed. "He has no right to trespass on my property and endanger my family!"

Katie wrapped her robe around herself more tightly. "Shouldn't we call the police? Make a report?"

"No." Walter said firmly. "No police."

"But, I got a pretty good look at him." She protested. "I could give the police a good description and they could"

"No police." Walter turned and headed back toward the house. "I don't need one more reason for Marcus Jones to be in my business."

Katie looked at Bill questioningly. "Bill...?"

Bill furrowed his brow and spoke quietly, so that Walter didn't hear. "Wouldn't do any good."

"Of course it would." She insisted. "I can give a description and the police will make a report. Then, they will look for him."

"And do what?" Bill met her gaze tiredly.

She shrugged, unsure of what he was getting at. "Arrest him?"

"Arrest him for what?" He shone the flashlight once more around the lawn. He didn't seem so much resistant to her idea as he was cynical.

"I don't know. Trespassing?" She was starting to feel the energy drain out of her argument. "Harassment?"

Bill shook his head. "The cops have bigger worries, believe me."

"Clarissa is only fifteen." Katie argued. "Surely the police would be concerned about that."

"Yeah, they would take your statement." He paused, as if he were thinking hard about what he was about to say. He was locked in some sort of mental debate with himself. Then, his mouth twisted into an even deeper, even sadder frown. "Listen, when I told you Marcus Jones thinks Walter killed Diedre..."

She nodded for him to continue.

"That wasn't all." Bill was hesitant, troubled. "Let's just say, the less Walter sees of Marcus Jones, the better for everyone."

"But don't you think we should at least..." She trailed off at the sight of Bill's uneasiness.

"There have been a couple of murders." He said finally. "Just like Diedre."

Katie blinked, shocked. "And the police think Walter is responsible?"

"But he's not." Bill said quickly. "He's not."

Katie nodded slowly, trying to process the information without the confusion, fear, and sadness that was trying to hijack her thoughts.

"It's because the victims worked for Walter or stayed in his hotels. Really loose connections, Katie." Bill was adamant. "If it were anyone else, Marcus Jones would never make the link."

Katie chewed her lip. The police thought he was a killer. But everyone who really knew him, loved him. How could she rationalize two such disparate opinions? Could so many people be wrong about him? Surely there must be more than just circumstantial evidence for the police to be so interested. And what about Walter's family, his friends? Were they just blinded by love and loyalty?

"I know you don't know him very well. You don't know any of us very well." Bill's eyes pleaded. "But you know us well enough to know Walter's not a killer."

Katie searched her own heart, then nodded. She did know that.

"And you know I wouldn't lie to you." He nodded, as well. "So believe me when I say I know Walter is innocent."

"Okay." She nodded slightly. "I know it, too. But we should still file a police report."

Bill scanned her face, maybe trying to verify her allegiance. Finally, he shrugged. "Walter says no. So, what can we do?"

Then he took Katie's arm and led her back to the house.

# Chapter Seven

It was a long time before Katie could fall asleep again. Her mind was racing with all kinds of thingsthe young man in the garden, Clarissa, Mom, and Grandma. She tried in vain to distract herself away from those thoughts long enough to fall asleep. In the end, she was only able to drop off because she was so exhausted.

But in her dreams, she was looking down at the backyard, from the window again. The garden was as beforesilent, lit only by moonlight. However, once again she sensed something else in the dark, a presence. She leaned closer to the window, scanning the shrubbery with her eyes, looking for something in the darkness, something wrong.

Her breath fogged the glass pane in front of her face, obscuring her vision. Then, beyond the opaque lens of the window, she thought she could see movement below. She reached out to wipe the fog from the glass and her hand inexplicably passed through the window. Yet, she wasn't surprised by this. It seemed to most natural thing in the world that her hand should not be stopped by anything solid. She stretched her hand out even further, until her whole arm was outside the window. Curious, she leaned forward, let her body pass through the glass.

Then, she was in the night air, above the patio. Her hair fluttered about her face and she brushed it back with one hand, so she could see the ground two stories beneath her. The cool autumn breeze churned her nightgown against her legs and the sound of the thin cotton flapping against body created a counter rhythm to the rustle of dried leaves on the ground and the swish of the arborvitae and boxwoods below.

She floated, two stories up, unconcerned about the fact that she was floating, or how she was floating, or even why. Her only interest was in searching the darkness, in locating the source of her anxiety—this presence, this feeling of casual malevolence. She stared down into the shadows cast by the landscaping, shadows on shadows of bushes, trees, sculptures.

The slightest movement in the bushes drew her attention and she fixed her eyes on it, trying to determine the source. She peered deeper into the darkness as her body drifted downward. As she approached the shadowy hedge, she thought she could make out a darker part of the blackness. But could that be right? Or was it simply that her eyes were straining, trying to find something when nothing was there?

She could almost make out a shape, almost see a movement, as she drifted so close to a row of tall bushes that she could nearly touch them. But as she extended her hand in front of her, it passed through the plants, the same as it had passed through the window. And now, confident, she let her head follow to the other side…

…until she was face to face with the man from before. His eyes widened slightly in surprise, then they narrowed and a fiendish grin stretched his lips, exposing two long, sharp incisors. He leaned toward her and wagged his tongue between those fangs in a disgusting, terrifying, and most certainly personal insult. Katie gasped and threw herself back from him.

She awoke with a sudden jerk, heart pounding and breath short, in her own bed. It took several seconds before she could believe she was safe. The dream had been so real, so intense, that even knowing it was only a product of stress and worry, she still feared the man with the teeth.

Katie sighed. There would be no sleep tonight. She knew that she would see that face every time she closed her eyes, even for a second. She threw off the blanket and got up. It would be quite some time before the children were up and ready for lessons. It was hours before sunrise, even. She would have to find some way to occupy her mind, keep her from thinking of that horrible dream.

"Maybe a book in the library." She thought, as she padded down the stairs in her bare feet. She had yet to fully explore all the shelves.

She worried a little that she would get turned around in the darkened big house. It occurred to her when she was halfway down the steps that she didn't exactly know where all the light switches were located. But the motion activated baseboard lights turned on as she approached them, and she didn't need the overhead lighting to find her way. When she reached the bottom of the steps, a look down the hall told her someone had left a light on in the library.

Katie made her way down the hall, past the kitchen, to the library. As she neared, she heard music playing softly from inside. It was soft enough that she couldn't quite determine what kind of music it was, what kind of instruments were playing, or even whether or not there were vocals. She slowed her steps and strained her ears.

It was unusual, that there would be music playing in the middle of the night. Unusual too, that there was music at all. She had never noticed Walter listening to music of any kind since she'd been here. She was not even aware of any devices in the libraryno radio, tv, or cd player.

Of course, Walter or Bill could be listening to something on their phone or on one of the laptops. Or, one of the children could have come down here, stealthily violating bedtime. Katie put one hand on the slightly ajar door and pushed.

"Hello?" She entered the room carefully and looked around.

"Well, hello." A man's voice said from behind her. She turned to see Adrian Chesterfield, standing in the doorway.

He was dressed in the same suit he had been wearing when they met, but the tie was undone and hanging loose around his collar. He was standing close enough she could smell his cologne, a woodsy, musky scent that shot straight through her senses and dinged her brain. She breathed him in, deeply and satisfyingly, without even realizing that she was doing it.

Her thoughts rushed, a torrent of senses through her head that both confused and excited her. He was standing close to her, so close. She lifted her eyes to his lips, half smiling and looking as though he were about to speak. She traced the faint line of a five o'clock shadow on his jawline. Thatshe couldn't even call it stubblethat slight darkening of complexion was not enough to mar his perfect skin or detract from his look in the least. In fact, it gave him a ruggedness that was very, very attractive.

She imagined how it would feel to graze his cheek with her own, feel the tiny frictions of his skin against her skin. She imagined being closer still, close enough to lose herself in that touch, in the masculine scent of his body. It was all she could do to keep her hand from reaching out on its own to caress his face, his hair, his chest. She...

He was looking at her as if he could read her mind and her thoughts made him smilea not at all polite smile. It was a smile that said he was thinking similar thoughts about her. Or worse.

"I..." She stammered, aware now that she was standing close enough to him that she could feel his body heat through the thin material of her nightgown. Even more shocking, she was aware that she was standing there in only her nightgown and felt no embarrassment or awkwardness. Instead, she was almost excited by that awareness. "I didn't know you'd be here."

"Of course you didn't." He drew her into his arms, enveloped her in a sweet, yet sensual embrace. He buried his nose in her hair murmuring something in her ear that she wasn't quite sure she even understood it to be words.

She knew, on some level, that she was acting counter to her personality, her morals, and her best interests. This was dangerous behavior, and it could cost her everything. Yet, she had no way of stopping herself from acting in this manner. Her skin was flushed and sensitive. Every touch of his fingertips, every breath in her ear, shot electricity through veins and made her crave more touches and more breaths. She wrapped her arms around him, sliding her hands up under his jacket.

Adrian said nothing, but his breathing, his subvocalizations were encouragement enough and she clung to him with an ardor that bordered on obsession. Her heart pounded, hard and fast, and she could feel it beat against his chest as he held her. He slid his lips along the slope of her neck, sending lightning bolts of heat throughout her whole body. Katie tilted her head, exposing her throat to him even more. Her hands moved down, tugged his shirt from his pants. Her breath was shallow with excitement.

She could feel Adrian's lips curl into a grin as he moved along her throat to her collarbone, then lower. His hand found its way to her breast and his fingers stroked her nipple through the cotton fabric of her nightgown, making her moan softly. The sound elicited a response from Adrian, a grunt of passion or of satisfaction.

The music, so quiet when she walked into the room, now seemed loud, almost overpowering. If Walter or Bill heard it and came to inv estigate... She burned with shame and guilt, but those feeling only enhanced her other sensations. She squeezed her fingers into his shoulders, gripping him tightly as she burned. Adrian ran both hands up under her gown, cupping her bottom and lifting her up to him.

"Yes." She whispered in his ear as he carried her to the closest table. Or maybe she hadn't voiced it at all? Maybe she had only thought I want this as her body betrayed every logical thought she had ever had. It was crazy that she should be doing this, that she should want this more than any other thing she had ever wanted. It was crazy that she didn't even care whether she had said it or thought it or shouted it from the rooftop. It was crazy and she desperately wanted this kind of crazy, and right now.

She fastened her lips on his and she could feel his smile against her as she kissed him without reservation. She felt the weight of his chest on hers as he eased her back onto the table, the heat of his body. His tongue found its way into her mouth, brushing her lips and exciting them to eager fullness. Then he was pushing beyond to stroke her pallet, push even deeper. This carnal invasion was experienced and welcomed by her whole body, and she could feel him hard and hot, pressed against her and poised just outsi--

She almost didn't recognize the alarm going off beside the bed, and it was even more difficult to understand what was happening. But then, her eyes opened and she was in bed in her room. Her heart still pounded, her blood still boiled and churned. But she knew that none of that had actually happened. She was as much disappointed as she was relieved.

She sighed, feeling very much ashamed to have had a sexy dream about a man she had met one time for about five minutes, and touched the off button on the alarm. She would have to make it a cold shower this morning.

# Chapter Eight

"Bill?" Katie stood over Bill, snoring softly on the couch. She raised her voice slightly. "Bill, are you asleep?"

Bill didn't stir in the least. He lay, exhausted, with one arm thrown over his eyes and the other hanging off the edge of the couch. One leg was up on the arm of the sofa and she could see the dirty scuff of his boot on the fabric. His mouth was open.

"Bill? Wake up." She touched his shoulder and he jerked awake violently. His eyes snapped open, and he looked around the room so wildly confused she instantly felt bad for disturbing him.

"No. Not asleep. I was just..." Bill sat up groggily and yawned. "Just resting my eyes."

"It's ok. Mr. Barrington is in his study and the kids are upstairs making their beds." Katie kept her voice low. "I'm sorry. I know you're tired. I just wanted to talk with you while we had a chance."

Bill rubbed his face, tried to wake up a little. "Sure, what's up?"

"That guy from the other night... I just have the weirdest feeling about him." Katie frowned. "I don't feel right about not calling the police."

"Weird feeling?" Bill shook the arm that had been hanging over the sofa, trying to get some feeling back into it. She wasn't sure he was fully awake yet. "Weird, how?"

"I don't know." She sighed. Maybe she shouldn't have awakened Bill. Walter had him standing guard every night, all night. Maybe she should have just called and made a police report. Surely, in the light of day, she would be able to make Walter see reason. "Weird, like I get the feeling he wanted something very bad for Clarissa."

"Yeah. I get that, too." Bill looked a little more engaged now. He moved over on the couch so she could sit. "Like more than just a teenage boy trying to get a teenage girl to sneak around with him at night."

"Exactly. There was just something about him, something about his manner." She shook her head, hesitated to say. After all, it was just a feeling, nothing concrete. But every instinct recoiled at the memory of his face in real life and in her dream. "He looked right at me, Bill."

Bill leaned forward. "Yeah?"

"Yes. He was standing down in the garden, looking up at me in the window." She remembered dream floating through that window to come face to face with him him and his lewd gesture. "He looked right at me and kind of... smiled."

"What?" Bill narrowed his eyes. "Like a hitting on you smile?"

She shook her head. The memory of his smile disgusted her. The memory of her dream disgusted her even more. "No. Like a you can't stop me smile."

"Little prick." He growled and his hands became fists.

"It was definitely not the look a teenager would give. It seemed older, more adult. More... sinister." She lowered her voice. "He gives me the creeps, Bill. Serious creeps."

Bill stood and walked a few steps away. He ran his hands over a wooden sculpture near the bookshelf, deep in thought, as if he were trying to decide on what to say. "I don't like the way he was able to get away so easily, either. We should have seen him leaving, at least. Or some evidence that he was there. There weren't even any footprints in the grass. No car nearby. Nothing."

Katie agreed. "And Clarissa..."

He narrowed his eyes. "What about her?"

"Before I stopped her, she was just looking out the window." She sighed, remembering the girl's blank look. "Almost as if she were in some kind of trance."

Bill frowned. He looked down at his hands, thinking again. "You remember when I asked you if you believed in the supernatural?"

"Bill I..." She trailed off. She was picturing the guy from the garden, the guy from her dream, and that horrible look he gave her. The image of his tongue vulgarly wagging between those pointed teeth... She shuddered involuntarily. "What do you want me to say?"

He looked up uncomfortably. "Well, think about it."

"Think about what?" She shook her head. This was exactly what she had been thinking for the last few days. But she couldn't say it out loud. "What are you saying? That this guy is some kind of supernatural creature?"

"Well, what if he is?" Bill shrugged. "You said yourself he gave you the creeps. Like he seemed like someone just pretending to be a teenage boy."

"I know, but..." A cold pit formed in her stomach. She knew what he was saying, but what he was saying was crazy. Wasn't it? "Bill, you can't be serious."

"Think about it. This guy only shows up at night. Clarissa shows up with bite marks on her neck. And she's looking more and more pale, like the blood is being drained from her." Bill raised his eyebrows and she silently hoped he wouldn't say what she thought he would say. "I think he might be a vampire."

"That's crazy." She laughed humorlessly. He had said it and she knew he was right. But he couldn't be right. Right? "I mean, yes. If there were such things as vampires, then I would say you might be right."

"Clarissa was staring out the window like she was in a trance." Bill challenged. "That was your phrase. A trance."

Memories of childhood terrors in front of the TV set flooded in. "Yes, but..."

"The bites on her neck showed up at exactly the same time he showed up." Bill nodded. "And exactly the same time she started looking pale and sick."

"I know it seems like it all fits. It's just..." Katie tried to slow this train of thought down. It was surreal, frightening, and repulsive, all at the same time. There must be some other, logical explanation for all of it. "Bill, it just sounds crazy."

"Oh trust me. I know how crazy it sounds. But believe me, it's not the craziest thing going on around here." Bill raised his eyebrows significantly. "Not even close."

Katie looked down at her feet. "So, suppose there are such things as vampires, and this guy really is one? What can we do about it?"

"What do you know about vampires?" Bill said softly.

"Well, I've only seen just about every vampire movie ever made." Katie was almost sick at the memory of Mom forcing her to watch horror movies every time she mentioned seeing Grandma. "They drink blood. You have to invite them into your house." Katie sighed. "They hate garlic and crosses. They can only come out at night."

"And what's the most important part?" Bill crossed to where she sat, looked her in the eyes.

Katie hesitated. She knew what Bill wanted her to say. It was just too awful to say. She shook her head.

"Everyone knows it." He urged.

She mumbled. "They can only be killed by a wooden stake through the heart."

Bill nodded. "Exactly."

"You can't possibly be suggesting we kill a man, a teenager." Katie looked at him incredulously. Every logical part of her brain rebelled against such a horrific idea. Yet, every instinct confirmed its truth. "That's insane."

"I'm not suggesting we kill a man or a boy." Bill said quietly. "I'm saying we kill a thing, a monster."

"I can't believe we're actually discussing this." Katie stood. She clasped her hands in front of her to stop them from shaking. "As if it were something that was really going to happen."

"Katie, this family has been through enough. I can't let something bad happen to Clarissa. Not when I can stop it." Bill said firmly. "I owe Walter that much."

"But kill him? Bill, that's crazy. That's murder." She grabbed his arm. "You're just going to walk up to him and stab him in the chest with a stake? What if someone sees? What if the kids see?"

"Obviously, I won't do it when anyone else is around." Bill rolled his eyes. "I'll find his lair. Then I'll get him during the day, while he's asleep."

"Lair?" Katie shook her head. "I can't believe this is happening. It's so unreal."

Bill shrugged. "Like I said, it's not even close to the craziest thing that's happened here."

"This is so..." Katie's voice trailed off. He was right. There were crazy things happening here. She had seen them herself. "There's something else."

He braced himself. "What is it?"

"I know Miss Bonham had... issues, but..." She hesitated. Could she trust Bill? Of course, he was just talking about killing vampires. "Maybe Miss Bonham wasn't as crazy as everyone seems to think. I mean, I've heard things, too."

Bill stared. His tone was cautious. "What kind of things?"

"I've heard voices at night." She said. "Well, a voice. A woman's voice."

Bill was silent for almost a minute. Then he nodded. "Yeah. I figured you did."

"You believe me?" Relief flooded through her. No one outside of this house had ever believed her when she told them.

"Sure. Why not? Like I said, it's not the weirdest thing going on around here." Bill shrugged. "Look, there have been ghost stories about this place for as long as I can remember. I told you about my Grandpa Bob's story about the ghost that drowns kids in the pond. You gotta think there's a kernel of truth in all that, right?"

Katie nodded. "Still, I know what everyone thinks of poor Miss Bonham. Please don't tell anyone about it, okay?"

"I won't." He nodded.

"Especially not Mr. Barrington." Katie said uneasily. "I don't want to get fired."

"Don't worry, Katie. Your secret's safe with me." Bill sighed sadly. "We've all got our secrets here."

"What secrets?" A woman entered the room with a vacuum cleaner. "Something I should know about, Bill?"

The woman, a forty-something brunette, wearing overalls, blue eye shadow, and a whole lot of jewelry, zeroed in on the dirty spot on the sofa and gave Bill a sour look. It was clear she didn't like him.

"Nobody said anything about secrets, Ravensong." Bill said, equally disgusted by her. He brushed past her and out of the room quickly. "You're imagining things."

"Hmph." The woman frowned a little. She looked Katie up and down. "And you are?"

"Hi. I'm Katie Gallagher." Katie held out her hand. "I'm the new nanny."

That seemed to perk the woman up. She came closer, took Katie's hand. She didn't so much shake it as she held it. Then she smiled, and the expression softened her face considerably. "Yes, I see that. It's nice to finally meet you. I'm Ravensong."

"It's nice to meet you, Miss Song." Katie gave her hand a quick shake and then withdrew it. "Are you the housekeeper Mr. Barrington told me about?"

"I must be." She laughed. "And it's Ravensong. That's my first name. Ravensong Music."

"Oh. I beg your pardon." Katie blushed. "I didn't realize."

"It's okay." Ravensong laughed. "My parents were what they used to call 'free spirits.' They gave me the name Ravensong to signify the power of light within me. Ravens, as you know, brought light to the world and delivered humankind from darkness."

"I didn't know that." Katie felt a little overwhelmed by the woman's spirited conversation, especially after such a dark discussion with Bill. She smiled awkwardly. "It's a lovely name."

"Is it?" The woman was distracted, examining Katie's face from all angles, with a strange smile on her lips. "You look just like her."

Ravensong reached toward her hair and Katie took a step backward. "Who?"

The movement snapped Ravensong out of her reverie and she withdrew her hand. "So, have you been making the children's beds this week?"

"No." Katie smiled. "They did."

"They did? Are you serious?" Ravensong laughed out loud, as if it were the most ridiculous story she had ever heard.

"Yes. Children need responsibilities." Katie was defensive of her work. "They need to learn to take care of their things and themselves."

Ravensong stopped laughing. She raised her eyebrows and nodded. "That's more work this week than these children have ever done in their lives."

"They haven't had much direction lately." Katie frowned a little, defensive now of her charges. "Miss Music, what did you mean when you said I looked like her? Like whom?"

"It's Ravensong, please." She smiled warmly and took Katie's hand in her own again. "Elizabeth. You are the spirit and image of your grandmother."

Katie nearly gasped at that, until she reminded herself that Willow Grove was Grandma's hometown. She made her voice calm and slid her hand out of the other woman's. "You knew my grandma?"

"Oh, yes." Ravensong nodded happily. "I know her quite well."

Katie let her use of the present tense slide. "I'm happy to meet you."

"And your father, too. Good man." She continued. "Very strong. Very powerful. Such a great loss."

"Thank you." Katie forced a smile at the strange condolences. "I miss them both very much."

Ravensong smiled at that, but it was a strange smile and Katie wasn't sure of its meaning.

"Well, if you will excuse me, Miss MusicRavensong," Katie edged toward the door. "I should check on the children."

"Katie," Ravensong took her hand once more as she passed. "You can talk to me, you know."

"Thank you." Katie nodded and pulled her hand away. "Excuse me."

Ravensong smiled that same smile again. "I would understand a great many things other people might not."

"Excuse me." Katie moved past her and out of the room.

# Chapter Nine

"Very good, Delia." Katie looked over the girl's shoulder at her paper. "Keep working on your spelling list."

"Thank you, Miss Gallagher." Delia beamed. "Some of these words are too hard for me. But Arabella helps me."

Katie knelt beside her. She spoke softly. "Delia, is Arabella here right now?"

The little girl smiled slightly. "No, but I can hear her in my head sometimes if I really try."

That thought sent a chill up her spine. Katie forced a smile and put her hand on top of Delia's head gently. "Well, tell her to stay out of there. We need the space for learning!"

"You're funny, Miss Gallagher." Delia laughed.

"Miss Gallagher, I've finished my English assignment." Blake held up his paper, uncharacteristically excited.

He was grinning, an expression she'd not seen since she got here. His eyes were bright and lively as she took his paper and returned his smile. "Well then, I will take a look at it and see how you did."

As soon as the page left his hand, however, his confidence faded. He frowned as Katie's eyes moved over the page. "I probably messed it up. I'm not very good at school."

"Blake, that's not true! This is very good." She smiled as she read. His writing had an enthusiasm, an energy, that must be hidden within his heart. If only she could find a way to bring it out into the open. "You've done very well, just in the week that I've been here."

Blake seemed to reluctantly cheer up. "Well... okay."

Katie watched as the boy warred with his own emotions, as if he wanted to be happy but was afraid to. She needed to find a way to raise Blake's self-esteem.

Clarissa stood and handed Katie a few pages. "I finished my writing assignment, too."

"Really?" Katie was pleasantly surprised. "You wrote a five-page story already?"

Clarissa smiled unkindly. "I was inspired."

"That's fantastic!" Katie looked over the pages. There were five full pages of scriptno space gobbling tricks like wide margins, large writing, or blank lines, things other children in other households had tried to get away with. She was impressed. "I can't wait to read it!"

"Oh, you'll love it." Clarissa smirked. "It's about an unwanted nanny who just shows up one night."

"Oh?" Katie could not help the sting that word unwanted dealt her.

"And then she sticks her nose in everyone's business." Clarissa continued. "And tries to change the way everyone does things."

Katie tried not to show it bothered her. After all, Clarissa was working through a lot of emotions. She was a child and Katie was the adult here. She thinned her lips in a toothless smile. "Well, that sounds very interesting. How does it end?"

Clarissa shrugged. "You'll have to wait and see."

"Well, that's quite imaginative." Katie said. "I like the way you used a real-life situation and turned it into a fictional narrative. Very creative."

Clarissa frowned, unhappy with the response. "Whatever."

"No, I'm very excited." Katie insisted. She put the pages into her lesson plan book and tapped the cover reverently. "That shows me some very complex thought processes are going on and you're able to harness those thoughts effectively and artistically. I can't wait to see how you channel that passion into all your assignments."

Clarissa frowned, disappointed that her plan to intimidate Katie was backfiring so profoundly. "Whatever."

"Oh no. I'm serious. Such a vivid imagination should be encouraged." Katie smiled broadly. "And who knows? You might really enjoy writing."

"Whatever." Clarissa sighed. "Are we done here?"

Katie raised her eyebrows in challenge. "Are we?"

Clarissa rolled her eyes and headed toward the door.

"Remember to read Chapter Three for tomorrow." Katie gestured back to the table, where Clarissa had left her books. "I will want to get your opinion on what the author was really trying to say in that chapter."

Clarissa sighed and headed back to the table for her books. "Fine."

"And clean up your workspace before you leave." Katie added.

Clarissa grumbled, but she did as she was told.

At the other table, Blake and Delia smiled to themselves and continued their writing assignments. Katie smiled down at them. They were adapting quickly to her presence, but she had to find a way to get through to Clarissa.

Katie scrolled down on her tablet, her eyes tired from staring at the screen so long. The internet was such a huge trove of information, sometimes she just got lost in it. She had started out reading about grief counseling for children, which progressed to art therapy. Then, she read some interesting articles about analyzing children's artwork to gain insight into their psychology.

From there, she read about childhood fears and trauma. And then she was reading about children who said they had seen ghosts or communicated with ghosts. Then, there was article after article about ghosts who intervened in a child's life to give them some message that would guide them, and sometimes even save their lives.

Suddenly, Katie realized that she had somehow shifted her focus from what was going on with the Barrington children to what had happened to her as a child. That realization was both startling and disturbing. She had learned a long time ago that seeing Grandma was just how her child brain processed the loss. Or, rather, she had tried to learn that. Mom had said Katie was hurting herself by clinging to a delusion, that she was hurting her with it, too. Grandma was gone. She couldn't talk to Katie or anyone else. She could not appear in her bedroom and try to give her a message.

Except, Katie knew that she did. She knew Grandma was gone, but also not gone. She knew Grandma could not be with her, but also that she did visit Katie. She knew Grandma was trying to tell her something important. But she also knew that she didn't want to hurt Mom, and so she had learned to pretend not to see Grandma's ghost.

Until she really didn't see her anymore. Katie set the tablet on the nightstand and turned off the light. She sighed.

What had Ravensong said about her Grandmother? I know her very well. Know her. Present tense. But Grandma had been gone for over 20 years. She couldn't possibly know Grandma. She had misspoken. Why was Katie so fixated on a simple error in speech, anyway?

Because. What if Grandma appeared to Ravensong, the way she had appeared to Katie? What if Grandma had given up on Katie, after Katie turned away from her? What if Ravensong was the one Grandma loved now?

No, Grandma loved her. Even if Katie had rejected the idea of communication with her spirit. Grandma would not have given up on her. She closed her eyes and tried to remember Grandma, as she was when she was alive. She could almost picture her, singing her strange, silly songs, and teaching Katie to write in their special code.

"One, two. The light in you." Katie whispered, suddenly remembering a counting rhyme she had learned as a child. "Three, four. An open door."

The memory of saying this little poem with Grandma flooded in, along with a host of emotion. She tried to remember the next lines but couldn't. It was likely something Grandma had made up, that no one knew except the two of them. And now, if she couldn't remember, that part of Grandma would be lost forever.

"Three, four. An open door." Katie repeated, but her memory was not jarred. She squeezed her eyes shut and tears fled the corners. "Three, four. An open door."

She could not remember.

Five-year-old Katie walked into the kitchen in the middle of the night. She wasn't sure what had drawn her there, but she knew she had to be there. She pulled a chair out of the kitchen table and sat down across from Grandma. The lights were still off, but the light from a nearly full moon shone through the window, illuminating the room well enough.

"Grandma!" Katie hopped up onto the chair. "I missed you!"

Grandma smiled and nodded. She opened her mouth to say something, but no sound came out. She looked a little frustrated and tried again.

"Can't you talk, Grandma?" Katie asked. "What's wrong?"

Grandma shook her head and smiled, to reassure her. Then she tried once more to speak, but the word came out very soft, almost too soft to hear.

"Katie.

# Chapter Ten

"Katie..." Softly, sadly. "Katie..."

Katie sat up in bed, grabbed her phone. Three a.m. She flipped on the light, looked around. The room was empty.

"Who is it? Who's there?" Katie opened the record app on her phone. If she could get proof that there was a ghost trying to communicate...

Well, she didn't know how that would help. But it would, at least, prove that she didn't imagine it. She held the phone up, panned around the room, trying to get the voice to speak again. "Hello? I want to help you. Where are you?"

Several minutes passed, but the voice didn't speak again. Katie shut off the recording and got up out of bed. She was ninety-nine percent sure she had heard the voice and wasn't just dreaming. It was a strange coincidence that she had been dreaming about Grandma trying to talk to her. Stranger still that she'd not had that dream in years, but she'd had it several times since coming to Willow Manor.

Of course, when it happened before, she wasn't asleep. She wasn't dreaming. Grandma was right there, trying unsuccessfully to talk to her. If she had been better at listening, if she could have somehow been more open to it, maybe, perhaps she would have heard Grandma's words. Perhaps she would have understood what Grandma wanted from her. Perhaps Grandma would still be talking to her.

Mom had tried to convince her for so long that Grandma had only been in her imagination, that her spirit never spoke to her. Even though Katie insisted, even though she knew in her heart it was real, she was only a child. Mom's threats of taking her to a doctor to "see what was wrong with her" or her punishments of hours of horror movies alone in the dark, weakened Katie's resolve to argue. Eventually, Mom won that argument, like she won all arguments. And Grandma stopped trying to talk to Katie.

Katie wrapped her bathrobe around herself and tried to push the guilt to the back of her mind. She knew that Grandma had come to her. She knew Grandma had spoken to her. But a small child was no match for her master manipulator mother. She would never know what information Grandma felt was important enough to try to communicate to her, even after death.

She tied the belt on the robe and stood a little straighter. Mom wasn't here now. And Katie wasn't a child. If this ghost had something to say, Katie was going to hear it. She quickly went to the door and stepped out into the hallway.

"Hello?" She whispered, so as not to wake everyone up. "Please tell me what you want."

"Katie..." She heard it softly, coming from the stairs.

Katie walked to the head of the stairs. She was strong. She would not back down from what was happening. "Please tell me how to help you."

The ghostly voice did not answer. She made her way downstairs and paused in the landing before continuing down the hall. Then she saw a light on in the study. Her dream about Adrian Chesterfield came rushing back to her, made her blush despite herself.

"Don't be silly, Katie." She silently chided herself and moved toward the study. "It was just a dream."

Still, the memory of Adrian's body against hers, dream or not, lingered. It made her heart beat fast. She peeked through the half open door. She could see Walter's desk, the lamp at its edge giving the room a soft glow. The smoke from a cigar resting in an ashtray circled the lamp. A man's hand held a crystal glass next to it.

Once again, memories of Adrian and the library played at the edges of her mind, warmed her blood. She stepped closer to the crack in the door, let her eyes trace the dark hair on the back of the hand. The fingers, strong and well-formed, gripped the glass so tightly Katie wondered that it didn't break from the tension its owner obviously felt.

"Hello?" Katie pushed the door open enough to walk through. Some wicked part of her mind still anticipated Adrian Chesterfield sitting at the desk.

Walter looked up as she entered. "Katie. What are you doing up at this hour?"

"I'm sorry to disturb you, Mr. Barrington." She breathed a sigh of both relief and disappointment. "I didn't realize anyone was in here."

"It's quite alright, Katie." He extinguished the cigar and waved the smoke away with his hand. "I just like the quiet here."

"It is very quiet here." She nodded. Her eyes traveled to the two fingers of scotch in his glass. "Is something wrong?"

"Yes, of course." He frowned bitterly. "It's all wrong."

"What do you mean?" She sat down in the chair in front of the desk. He looked almost spiritually beaten. "What's wrong?"

Walter slammed back the scotch and gazed into the glass as if he expected there to be more. He sighed. "Nothing. I'm just upset."

Katie tried to meet his eyes, but he didn't look up from the glass. "Can I help?"

Walter laughed bitterly. "What could you possibly do, my dear, that would help in the least?"

"I don't know. Listen?" Katie tried to shrug off the halfhearted dismissal. Of course, he didn't mean to hurt her feelings. She reached across the desk and touched his hand gently. "It seems like something is really bothering you. Talking might make you feel better."

"I'm sorry, Katie." He sighed and met her gaze. "I'm being very rude, and you are being very kind. Thank you."

"I just hate to see you like this." She said softly.

Walter sighed and nodded. He pulled his hand from under hers and rubbed his face tiredly. "I suppose you'll only see it on the news anyway."

"The news?" She leaned back, slightly alarmed. "What's happened?"

"I assume you know the Barringtons made their fortune in the hotel business?" He said.

"Yes." She nodded. "All those fancy hotels up and down the coast."

"Yes. And I assume you know that the hotel business is very fickle." Walter frowned and turned one palm up as if to say it was all out of his hands. "One bad review can be devastating."

"I see." She nodded. "And did you get a bad review for one of your hotels?"

Walter laughed so cynically she drew back a little. "I suppose the reviewer might have given us a bad review... if he hadn't been murdered in his room last night."

"Murdered?" Katie gasped.

"Yes. Gruesomely murdered." Walter's face twisted with disgust. "His throat was torn out."

"Oh my God!" Katie put a hand to her own throat self-consciously. "That's horrifying!"

"Yes. And that's not the half of it." Walter drew another glass and the bottle of scotch from the desk drawer and uncapped it. He poured a little in both glasses, then passed one to Katie. "There have been similar murders in the countryside between here and the town."

"I..." Katie took the glass and gazed down at the amber liquid. "I know about them."

"What?!" Walter seemed shocked. But he quickly resigned himself to the fact. "Well, of course. Why wouldn't you have heard all the stories? I suppose then my only question is, why are you still here?"

Katie frowned. "What do you mean?"

Walter took a sip and stared off into the room before answering. "The whole town thinks I'm responsible."

"That's crazy." Katie said. "It's not your fault. Any of it."

"You don't know that, Katie." Walter put the glass down on the desk, pushed it away from him. "If you had any sense, you'd just run. Far and fast, away from Willow Manor."

Katie held her glass with both hands, stared into the reflected lamp-light on its surface. So many people had tried to warn her away from Willow Manor, just in the short time she had been here. It made her wonder if half the danger people were warning her against was real.

"That's no way to talk." She put her untouched glass on the desk next to Walter's. "What would your children think, if they heard you talking like that?"

Walter shook his head. He stood and crossed the room, stopping at a rustic wooden statue near the window. He ran his hands over the wood and spoke softly, dejectedly. "I feel like I've failed them, as well. I failed to keep Diedre safe... Failed my stockholders and employees... And failed my children."

"You haven't failed anyone, Mr. Barrington. You have three fantastic children, who love you and need you." Katie tried to be encouraging. "And you must be good for your stockholders and employees. Otherwise, why would they stay? You aren't responsible for anyone's death. Not your wife's. Not your employees'. Certainly not that reviewer's."

"I don't know about that. The killer is clearly targeting those around me." Walter turned and shook his head sadly. "It's very much personal. I just can't figure out why."

"Personal?" Katie didn't see how it could be. "Why would you say that?"

"Because of this." Walter walked over, picked his cell phone up from the desk, and opened the photo app. He showed it to her. It was a photo of a handwritten note laying on the floor next to a pool of blood. "It was addressed to me personally."

Katie read the note:

Walter Gerard Barrington

Release my property or more will die!!!

"Release my property?" Katie knit her brow. "What property?"

"I don't know. It doesn't make any sense." Walter smiled derisively and sat back down at the desk. "But they used my full name and three exclamation points, so you have to assume they're serious about it."

She passed the phone back to him. "Have you told the police about it?"

"Yes. It's being investigated." Walter air quoted the word investigated. "But I know that Marcus Jones is not interested in anything that doesn't fit his narrative."

"That you are the killer?" Katie finished.

"Yes." Walter picked up the half-empty glass and drained it. "He seems to only want to consider evidence that supports that idea."

"That can't be true." Katie frowned. "Why would he be like that?"

"It probably has something to do with our personal history." Walter nodded. "Marcus Jones was engaged to my wife. She broke up with him when she met me."

Katie nodded. Now it made sense why the two men did not like each other. No wonder Walter did not want to involve Marcus Jones the other night with Clarissa. Still, Officer Jones was a law enforcement professional. Would he really jeopardize his career and ignore physical evidence, as Walter was suggesting?

"Surely he can't be holding that against you for so long?" She reasoned. "That had to have been nearly twenty years ago."

One side of Walter's mouth quirked up, as if he could not believe she was so naïve. "You should go to bed, Katie. Tomorrow is a school day."

"You should get some rest, too." She stood slowly, feeling very useless that she wasn't able to help Walter. She cast her eyes around the room helplessly. "I wish I could help."

"Yes. Well." Walter sighed deeply and sadly. He looked off into the night outside the window.

"Please, Mr. Barrington. You need to get some sleep." She crossed the room and drew the curtains closed. "Things will be okay. I promise."

Walter did not smile. "How could you possibly promise that?"

"II don't know. I just know they will. We have to trust in that." She looked down at her bare feet as she spoke and her eyes lighted on the base of the wooden statue. There were three symbols carved into the block. She nearly gasped. "Where did you get this?"

"What? The art?" Walter's expression softened. "Diedre. She loved wood sculptures. Filled up the house with them."

Katie nodded. She had seen them in the children's rooms, as well as the living room and here. She just hadn't looked at them closely. Now that she did, she saw the symbolsand she saw, with astonishment, that she could read them.

"I think they're a little primitive for my taste." Walter smiled. "But my wife loved them so much. I can't bear to get rid of them."

The first symbol was protection. The second was love. This was the secret code Katie had shared with Grandma. How would Diedre Barrington know Grandma's secret code?

"This one, especially." Walter stared at it, remembering happier times. "She gave this one to me as a wedding present. It's one of my most prized possessions."

It was the third symbol that Katie didn't recognize. When she and Grandma wrote this code phrase, that was the spot she would put the symbol for her name. So, whose name was this third symbol, she wondered?

"I can see why it would be." Katie smiled, surprised, pleased, and curious. She touched the top of the statue reverently and headed toward the door. "Good night, Mr. Barrington."

9 798330 618521